W9-BTD-422

"I Told You—I Want A Divorce."

"That's not going to happen."

Zac's bronzed face was inscrutable. This was not the man she'd fallen in love with. This was someone else altogether. A man so hard she feared he'd break her.

As he'd already broken her heart.

"I can't believe I agreed to marry you!" Pandora was talking to herself as much as to him.

"That's too bad. Because we are going on our honeymoon, to be alone—like you wanted."

"No way!"

"Stop fighting me."

"Never," she vowed.

Dear Reader,

In my teens a wide variety of books about Greece enthralled me. Romances set on islands owned by gorgeous Greek heroes. Gerald Durrell's laugh-out-loud-funny autobiography, *My Family and Other Animals,* about growing up on the island of Corfu.

I devoured *The Odyssey* and, utterly fascinated, I went on to read tales of travelers who had followed in the wake of Odysseus. I loved Greek myths and legends—some of them were tragic, some were touching and almost all of them overflowed with passion and emotion. Among my favorites was Pandora's Box. So when I created my own Greek hero, Zac Kyriakos, and his heroine, Pandora Armstrong, I couldn't resist playing with this theme. What happens when you unwittingly start a process that you can't stop? Can you ever make it right again? And how can love ever survive such a setback?

I hope you enjoy reading *The Kyriakos Virgin Bride,* the first book in the BILLIONAIRE HEIRS miniseries. Please visit me at my Web site www.tessaradley.com to find out more about my upcoming books, including *The Apollonides Mistress Scandal,* on sale next month. I always love hearing from readers!

Take care,

Tessa

TESSA RADLEY

THE KYRIAKOS VIRGIN BRIDE

NORTH AUSTIN BRANCH
5724 W. NORTH AVE.
CHICAGO, IL 60639

Silhouette® Desire

Published by Silhouette Books
America's Publisher of Contemporary Romance

If you purchased this book without a cover you should be aware that this book is stolen property. It was reported as "unsold and destroyed" to the publisher, and neither the author nor the publisher has received any payment for this "stripped book."

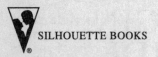

SILHOUETTE BOOKS

ISBN-13: 978-0-373-76822-6
ISBN-10:   0-373-76822-2

THE KYRIAKOS VIRGIN BRIDE

Copyright © 2007 by Tessa Radley

All rights reserved. Except for use in any review, the reproduction or utilization of this work in whole or in part in any form by any electronic, mechanical or other means, now known or hereafter invented, including xerography, photocopying and recording, or in any information storage or retrieval system, is forbidden without the written permission of the editorial office, Silhouette Books, 233 Broadway, New York, NY 10279 U.S.A.

This is a work of fiction. Names, characters, places and incidents are either the product of the author's imagination or are used fictitiously, and any resemblance to actual persons, living or dead, business establishments, events or locales is entirely coincidental.

This edition published by arrangement with Harlequin Books S.A.

® and TM are trademarks of Harlequin Books S.A., used under license. Trademarks indicated with ® are registered in the United States Patent and Trademark Office, the Canadian Trade Marks Office and in other countries.

Visit Silhouette Books at www.eHarlequin.com

Printed in U.S.A.

R0411820873

Books by Tessa Radley

Silhouette Desire

Black Widow Bride #1794
Rich Man's Revenge #1806
**The Kyriakos Virgin Bride* #1822

*Billionaire Heirs

TESSA RADLEY

loves traveling, reading and watching the world around her. As a teen Tessa wanted to be an intrepid foreign correspondent. But after completing a bachelor of arts and marrying her sweetheart, she became fascinated with law and ended up studying further and to become an attorney in a city practice.

A six-month break traveling through Australia with her family re-awoke the yen to write. And life as a writer suits her perfectly; traveling and reading count as research and as for analyzing the world…well, she can think *what if* all day long. When she's not reading, traveling or thinking about writing she's spending time with her husband, her two sons—or her zany and wonderful friends. You can contact Tessa through her Web site www.tessaradley.com.

For the hardworking hosties at eHarlequin.com—
some of whom I've known since I first started writing.
Rae, you held my hand when I needed it most.
Jayne, you're a cyber lifesaver. And Dee, Lori, Dream
and the rest of the team…you're all simply awesome!

To MJ and Karen, your guidance is always valued.
Thank you, always!

Tony, Alex and Andrew—where would I be without you
guys to keep me sane? And Karina Bliss, Abby Gaines
and Sandra Hyatt, you're fabulous friends.

One

"I do."

Pandora Armstrong spoke the vow in a clear, steady voice, and a warm tide of radiance swept over her. She sneaked a look up at her groom. Zac Kyriakos stood like a rock beside her, feet apart, facing the archbishop. Serious. Intent. Utterly gorgeous.

He was staring straight ahead. His profile could've been culled from any of the statues or friezes in the Acropolis Museum he'd taken Pandora to explore three days ago. The arrogant nose that ran in a straight sweep from his forehead to the nose tip, the strong jaw, the broad and high-boned cheekbones all resembled the marble statues she'd seen. But it was on his full mouth that her gaze lingered. Jeez, his mouth…

Full and sensuous, it was a mouth made for pure sin.

Zac glanced down and caught her staring. His colder-than-glass green eyes blazed, possessive. And that sexy to-die-for mouth curved into a smile.

Desire shot through her. Pandora tore her gaze away and stared blindly at the bouquet of creamy white roses clasped in her free hand.

Dear God. How could she feel like this about a man? And not just any man. This was Zac Kyriakos, who made her feel feverish and shaky. What had he done to her?

Enthralled her?

She blinked, fighting the urge to wipe her eyes, in case she woke up and discovered she'd dreamed the whole thing. How could she, Pandora, Miss Goody Two-Shoes—except for that terrible summer three years ago—have fallen in love so quickly?

Dimly she heard the archbishop say, "You may kiss the bride."

The vows and the kiss were not part of the Greek Orthodox ceremony. Zac had requested the traditional vows for her sake.

She was married!

Married to the tall, dark and exceedingly handsome man whose right hand she clutched so tightly that her fingernails must be leaving crescent-shaped marks on his palm. Inside, her stomach cramped with nervous excitement. It wasn't every day that a woman married a man who until three months ago had been a stranger.

"Pandora?"

She lifted her head. Their eyes connected. Heat arced between them. Zac's eyes smouldered. Possessive. Hungry. But there was a question in those compelling eyes, too.

Pandora nodded, a small, almost imperceptible nod, granting him the permission he sought.

Zac's hand tightened on hers. The warm weight of his other palm rested on the curve of her hip covered by the embroidered wedding gown passed from Kyriakos bride to Kyriakos bride through centuries. A gentle tug turned her to face him. His head swept down. That devastating mouth brushed hers, warm and intimate.

And just like that Pandora forgot about the archbishop, forgot about the people packed into the pews. Forgot that this was Zac Kyriakos. Shipping tycoon. Billionaire.

The only reality was the sensual touch of his lips on hers. And the heat that shivered through her.

Too soon he set her away. Only then did she become aware of the flashing cameras and remember they stood in a church where nearly a thousand people watched. Instantly the trembling heat evaporated. Despite the blazing white August sun outside, she felt suddenly chilled.

"Goodness!" Pandora's eyes stretched wide as she stared at the noisy wall of paparazzi surrounding the bridal car as they turned into Zac's estate in Kifissia, the exclusive area north of Athens where the reception was being held.

"Overwhelming?" A flash of white teeth and a wicked grin lit up Zac's darkly tanned face. "A three-ring circus?"

"Yes." Pandora leaned back, trying to hide from the intrusive camera lenses. From the minute she'd stepped off the plane the paparazzi had been waiting to mob her. But Zac and his bodyguards had kept the hungry horde at a distance. Pandora supposed she should have anticipated the curious speculation the wedding between Zac Kyriakos and a reclusive heiress had roused. The great-grandson of a Russian princess and the legendary Orestes Kyriakos, Zac had inherited most of his fortune from his grandfather, Socrates, after Orestes had used his kidnapped bride's wealth to restore the state of the Kyriakos fortune to its pre-Great War glory. Both Orestes and Socrates had been legends in their own times, and Zac himself featured prominently on the covers of the world's finance magazines, as well as making the annual list of most eligible bachelors in the known universe for the last decade.

But naively Pandora hadn't given his fame a thought, hadn't expected to have her wedding treated like that of royalty.

"Smile. They think our wedding is romantic. A modern fairy tale," Zac whispered into her ear. "And you're the beautiful princess."

Feeling as though she were performing to the gallery, Pandora turned to the window and bared her teeth in a travesty of a smile. The cameramen went crazy. And then they were sweeping through the tall wrought-iron gates, along the private tree-lined avenue through parklike gardens.

"Pandora." Without warning, Zac's expression turned serious and he reached for her hand. "Remember what I told you when you arrived? Don't read the papers. Don't search for those photos in the newspapers tomorrow. The lies and half-truths that accompany them will only upset you. Concentrate on us, on our future together," he said, his voice unexpectedly fierce as his thumb caressed the soft skin on the inside of her wrist. "The speculation, the gossip and garbage the tabloids dredge up will destroy you."

"I know. I already promised you I won't read the papers." She sighed. "I only wish Dad had been here." Her father's absence was the only shadow that hung over an otherwise perfect day. But since a bad bout of pneumonia four winters ago had left his lungs permanently damaged, necessitating regular doses of oxygen, her father no longer risked airline travel. "I always thought he'd be there on my wedding day to give me away."

The realization was dawning that she'd left her father and her childhood home far behind. After today, she would spend the rest of her life with Zac. Loved. Adored. The pomp and people didn't matter. Nothing mattered. Nothing except Zac.

Zac's house—more like a mansion, with its tower and stone walls—appeared before them. This would be her home from now on, together with the town house he owned in London. Zac had also spoken about buying a retreat in New Zealand, near her father's station.

"Your father may not be here, but I am. I'll always be here for you." At the intensity in his voice she turned her head. His hard, hewn features were softened by the sun filtering through the bulletproof glass windows, his eyes curiously gentle. Her throat tightened. She cast around for words but couldn't find any that matched the moment.

"Are you ready to face the world, *yineka mou?*" he asked as the car slowed.

My wife.

Pandora shot him a dazzling smile, happiness overflowing within her. She smoothed down the swathes of silk of the antique full-skirted gown.

"I'm ready for anything."

Zac helped her from the car and they braved the informal

honour guard of smiling well-wishers that lined the path to the front door. Pandora couldn't wait to meet Zac's friends, the sister and cousins he'd talked about incessantly during his stay in New Zealand. She'd wanted to meet them earlier in the week when she'd arrived in Athens. Zac had smiled, his eyes crinkling in that irresistible way that she loved, and told her he wasn't ready to share her yet. He wanted to play the tourist, he'd explained, to show her around. There'd be time enough to meet his friends and kin and staff later…at the wedding. She'd acquiesced. Zac only had to smile at her and she turned to mush.

They'd met at High Ridge, her father's vast sheep station in the South Island. Zac had come to New Zealand to discuss the possibility of guests flying in for exclusive stays at a working sheep station in luxury accommodation while a Kyriakos cruise ship docked at Christchurch.

And it had been at High Ridge that the miracle had taken place—Zac had fallen in love with her. A whirlwind courtship followed. Three weeks. Packed with precious hours spent together. Then he'd stunned her with his proposal of marriage, the fabulous diamond ring, the promise to cherish her forever.

Recklessly, she'd said yes. And started to cry. He'd wiped the happy tears away, and his tenderness had made her love him even more.

Her father had been over the moon when they'd broken the news. He'd pumped Zac's hand up and down.

And then Zac had jetted off back to Europe, back to running the billion-dollar shipping company he'd inherited from his grandfather. And, although an ocean had separated them, they'd spoken on the phone every day. Morning for him. Night for her in New Zealand. During those long conversations, Pandora had come to know the man she'd fallen in love with. There'd been two more lightning-swift visits. And, finally last week she'd flown to Athens for five days of playing tourist in the city with Zac at her side. It had all culminated in the Big Day.

Today.

Now, as they moved forward into the massive arched entrance of Zac's home accepting congratulations, Pandora recognised some of the faces. She was kissed on the cheek by a famous Hollywood actress and her equally famous husband, a singer in a rock band. Several legendary businessmen wished her and Zac well, and she smiled at a star footballer and his fashion-icon wife.

Inside the huge house she glimpsed a European prince and his popular Australian wife, a socialite who'd sprung to fame from a television-reality show, and several stunning supermodels stood out from the crowd. Pandora's sense of inadequacy grew.

Her mouth dry with nerves, she allowed Zac to lead her to the dais where the wedding table was set with silver cutlery and exquisite antique crockery.

And still the congratulations didn't stop. People streamed past the table in a blur of faces. There was no time for intimacy as distant members of Zac's family, his colleagues and acquaintances smiled at her, until Pandora was sure that everyone in the room wanted a good look at her.

Did she measure up? Or had they expected more from the woman Zac married? The thought was daunting.

She searched the crowded tables. Evie and Helen, two of her school friends from St. Catherine's, were out there somewhere. For a decade the girls had been cloistered together in the strict boarding school in the backcountry. Except for vacations, Pandora had spent most of her life at St. Catherine's until leaving a few months before her eighteenth birthday three years ago. Since then, apart from a couple of vacations with friends' families, she'd helped her father at High Ridge.

Pandora felt terrible that she hadn't had a chance to greet her friends. She would search them out later, she told herself, looking at the sheer number of people with worried eyes. Even if they didn't see her, they'd forgive her. Understand that tonight her priority was her husband.

"Here comes Basil Makrides with his wife, Daphne," Zac murmured. "He's a business associate."

Pandora turned to smile at the couple. After the Makrideses moved off, there was a small lull.

"Where's your sister? I haven't met her yet." Pandora had hoped to meet his sister before the wedding ceremony. Had craved company while the skilled hairdresser styled her hair and a makeup artist tended to her face and the dressmaker who'd altered the wedding dress fussed in the wardrobe. It would've been nice to have Zac's sister there…or even the cousin or aunt he'd spoken about. To assure herself that they would like her.

That she would get on with them.

Zac's face darkened. "My sister didn't make the wedding. There was a problem."

Pandora took in his tightly drawn mouth. "Is she…ill?" She probed carefully.

"Nothing like that." Zac's tone was abrupt. "It need not concern you. She'll be coming later."

Pandora stiffened. Zac never treated her like some silly little butterfly whose opinions didn't matter. What was going on here? Was this about her…or was there something about his sister—

"I'm sorry. I was too terse." Zac's voice interrupted her thoughts. "My brother-in-law is the problem—he's not an easy man to be married to."

"Oh, dear." Pandora drew her own conclusions. "Your poor sister, married to a brute."

"He doesn't beat her. It's nothing like that."

"Oh?" This time her tone was loaded with curiosity.

But Zac shook his head. "I don't want to think about my brother-in-law. Especially not on my wedding day. He makes me angry."

"We don't want that." Pandora rested a hand on his arm. "You tell me about it when you're ready."

"You are the perfect wife," Zac breathed and brushed a row of kisses across the exposed crest of her shoulder, causing the man and woman approaching the table to tease him mercilessly. A camera flashed. Pandora jumped.

"Don't worry," Zac murmured close to her ear. "Everyone here tonight has been invited—and vetted. There are no members of the press, only family and friends. Oh, and one professional photographer with a spotless reputation for discretion, who will capture memories of the occasion for us to enjoy."

The press? Pandora's stomach balled at the thought. She hadn't even considered them, with their avid hunger for pictures of her and Zac together.

During the interminable dinner that followed, cameras continued to flash while Zac introduced her to wave upon wave of strangers. Celebrities, business acquaintances, distant cousins, hobbling great-uncles. She could see the curiosity in the women's eyes, sense the men's speculation.

Why had Zac Kyriakos, given all the choice in the world, married a little nobody from New Zealand? It was a question which Pandora asked herself repeatedly but couldn't answer. At last she pushed away the nagging feeling that there was something she was missing and let Zac hold her close while he continued to introduce her to their guests.

The first waltz was over.

Pandora stared at the flushed stranger with the sparkling silver eyes in the mirror. Looking away, she picked up a jug and poured herself a glass of chilled water and drank greedily. She'd slipped away to check that her makeup was still intact…to make sure it would withstand the army of cameras that flashed like streaks of lightning across the crowded dance floor, capturing endless images of her and Zac as they circulated the room.

Stroking mascara onto her lashes, Pandora admitted to herself that she found the whole situation overwhelming. How could she explain that despite the enormously rich trust fund that she would come into when she was twenty-five, she found the glamour of Zac's world—with its famous faces, the constant stares and the unrelenting glare of the cameras—unnerving?

With a sigh, she dropped the tube into her bag and zipped it shut. A last sip of water, then she made her way back to the noise and bright lights and glitz.

"Pandora, over here," Zac called to her. His height

made him easy to find and Pandora threaded her way through the crowd.

"This is my *theos* Costas—my uncle, my mother's brother." Zac introduced her to the man at his side.

Pandora smiled at the older man. Cheery blue eyes twinkled down at her as he took her hand in his.

"The pleasure is all mine." He lifted her fingers to his lips and brushed a gallant kiss across the tips.

"My uncle is a renowned ladies' man, so take care." Zac laughed, his fondness for the older man evident. "I don't know how Aunt Sophia puts up with it."

Zac's uncle shrugged. "She knows she's the one I love." The simple words tugged at Pandora's heart. "You have already met my son."

Pandora struggled to think who Costas's son might be.

"Dimitri."

"Oh, yes." Relief filtered through her. Zac's cousin. "He's the lawyer who drew up the prenuptial and the *koum*—" she stumbled over the unfamiliar word "—best man," she amended, "who held the crowns over our heads during the ceremony."

"Koumbaro," Zac corrected.

"Yes, *koumbaro,*" she echoed the Greek word. Zac had explained that, as *koumbaro,* Dimitri would be godfather to their first child—one day. A wholly unfamiliar feminine quiver shot through her at the thought of a little boy with eyes like Zac. But first she wanted to spend a couple of years alone with her new husband.

"You learn our customs quickly." Costas looked satisfied. "It has been overwhelming? Meeting so many new people?"

She nodded, grateful for his understanding.

"You can call me *Theos*—uncle—like Zac does."

"Thank you, Theos. Zac speaks of you often." Pandora knew Zac's uncle had been a father figure to Zac during his teens. A lawyer by profession, Costas had taken an active role on the board of Kyriakos Shipping even though, as Zac's maternal uncle, he was not a Kyriakos himself. Only when Zac had gained control of the board had his uncle resigned to put all his energy back into his law firm, which he now ran with his daughter, Stacy, and his son, Dimitri. Dimitri ran the Athens office with his father, while Stacy worked in the London office, she recalled. Pandora remembered the respect and love with which Zac had spoken of his uncle during their long nightly transworld calls. "I'm so pleased to meet you," she said.

"We will talk more tomorrow," Theos Costas said. He clapped Zac on the shoulder. "Now, my boy, it is time to go dance with your bride."

"Hey, Zac, it's your turn to dance."

The call interrupted Pandora from asking what Costas meant by talking more tomorrow. She glanced around and saw two men approaching, grinning widely.

"Come, Zacharias."

Zac threw Pandora a rueful glance. "I was hoping to escape this."

"Not a chance." The taller of the men chuckled, his hawklike features alight with good humour.

Zac sighed dramatically. "Pandora, meet Tariq and Angelo—more of my cousins."

Pandora examined them with interest. Zac had spoken about both men with affection and admiration. When his grandfather, Socrates, had died, each of his three grandsons had inherited a sizeable part of his fortune. As the only son of the only son, Zac had inherited the biggest share. But Tariq and Angelo had been well provided for—as had Zac's sister.

Looking from one man to the other, Pandora could discern small similarities. Not only in the family resemblance in the cast of their features but also in the air of command each of the three radiated.

"Welcome to the family." It was Angelo who spoke. He had piercing eyes, the colour of the sea, and a crop of golden hair.

Pandora smiled. "Thank you."

Then Tariq took her by the shoulders and bestowed a kiss on each cheek. "Bring your husband and come and visit Zayad."

Give us some time alone first," Zac growled. "We'll visit in a couple of months."

Tariq grinned. "Take your time. Now you better go dance."

Zac whisked her off into a large adjoining room where the ensemble was now playing Greek music and guests swayed in seemingly never-ending counterclockwise spirals. At their appearance a shout went up.

"Zac, here, join in."

Dimitri beckoned to them.

An opening appeared in the hands. Zac pulled Pandora forward. Then they were part of the swaying, shuffling mass. For the first few minutes it was as if she had two left feet, and she struggled to find the steps to the dance, frowning as she watched Zac's feet beside her. Right step, cross, right foot point to the back, forward, shuffle and a little hop.

Suddenly the rhythm came, fitting to the strum of the bouzouki on the bandstand. Euphoria swept over her.

She could do this.

As Zac moved, her body mirrored his steps. As his arms went back, hers did, too. As he widened the circle, she went with him and the line behind followed. It was heady stuff.

The music quickened. Zac's steps quickened. Her feet danced faster and her breath came more rapidly. All around her she could hear a few of the guests singing along in Greek.

She wished she understood the lyrics.

Zac's hand enfolded her right hand, while on the left she linked hands with Dimitri. The person on the other side of him moved forward. Pandora caught the woman's eye and they exchanged hectic smiles, then Pandora was concentrating on her feet again, taking care not to lose the rhythm.

The music changed, became softer, slower. She stumbled, Zac's arm came around her, steadying her, then his hand slid down her arm and took her hand again. Heat shot through her. The steps had changed. A frown pleated her forehead. She bit the tip of her tongue and concentrated furiously.

"Let the music take you," Zac murmured. "Relax. Your body must be fluid like the tide in the sea, not stiff like driftwood."

Pandora missed the next step.

His fingers shifted under hers. "Loosen your grip on my hand. You're trying too hard. Listen to the music, feel it ebb and flow through your body."

Pandora concentrated on the plaintive wail of the singer's voice.

"She's singing about her love who went away." His voice was low. "Each day she waits at the wharf for his boat to return, she is sure he will come back for her."

The music caught Pandora up. Loss and grief filled the singer's voice. Tears thickened the back of Pandora's throat.

"That's right. Now you have it." Zac sounded triumphant.

Pandora jerked back to reality.

She was following the steps. "How on earth did that happen?" she asked, amazed.

"Greek music comes from the heart. The dancing translates the music. Your body must feel the music." His gaze held hers. "It is easy. It's about what you feel. Don't make it difficult by thinking about technique, about complex things. Just feel the emotion. The joy of love, the pain of betrayal. The steps will follow."

A warm flush of accomplishment filled her. The music flowed through her, her feet shifted, her body sequayed forward as she followed Zac.

Again the music changed.

The line broke apart.

Zac tugged her hand. "We'll sit this one out." A waiter materialised with a tray of champagne flutes and tall glasses of ice water. "Would you like a drink? Champagne?"

She was hot and thirsty from the effort of the dancing. "Just water, please."

Zac handed her a glass. She sipped, the ice bumping against her top lip. Placing the empty glass on a passing tray, she said, "That was wonderful."

"Come, let's go somewhere cooler." He guided her, skirting the edge of the room. "You picked up the steps easily."

She laughed up at him. "Not easily. You'll have to teach me more—when we're alone." If that ever happened.

His mouth curved. "Perhaps on our honeymoon, hmm?" He led her through the open French doors. Outside, the night air was warm and stars studded the black velvet sky. Zac reached up and tore off the bow tie and undid the top button of his shirt.

Her heartbeat picked up. "So we're going to have a honeymoon? Some time together? Totally alone?"

"Oh, yes." He leaned against a pillar and, reaching out, pulled her toward him, his eyes darkening. "Totally alone. I think we deserve it."

"Where are we going?"

"I will surprise you. Suffice to say there will be sun, sea and only Georgios and Maria, the couple who look after the villa."

Excitement thrummed through her. "I can't wait. When do we go?"

"Tomorrow," Zac's voice turned husky. "I, too, can't wait."

Inside, the music had stopped.

There was an instant of simmering silence. She could feel Zac's gaze, intense, waiting.

Waiting for her to move. To do something. Say something. She did not know what he expected. So she did what *she* wanted. She rose on tiptoe, pressed her lips against his...and the fire caught. Zac moaned, his lips parting under hers.

His mouth was hot and hungry.

Distantly she could hear the next song starting. She blocked it all out. And concentrated on Zac. On that taunting, teasing mouth that she couldn't get enough of.

Then Zac was straightening. "This isn't the place for this. Anyone could see us. Come." He tugged her hand.

"Zac, we can't just leave," Pandora protested, casting a frantic glance back inside.

"Of course we can." He stopped. His gaze was hot, stripping away thought, leaving nothing but a raw awareness of his strength, his masculinity. Perspiration added a sexy sheen to those sculpted cheekbones and his mouth curved in a wickedly hungry smile. "Why should we stay one more minute when we both want to leave?"

"Because…" Pandora tried to summon her objections, to search desperately for a reason. But all she could think of was the way the silk shirt clung to his damp body. *His body.* Staring at the bare slice of skin at his throat, she swallowed, then said halfheartedly, "Because it's our wedding and we haven't cut the cake."

He shrugged. "The cake can wait. We can cut it at lunch tomorrow. Now come." Zac gave her hand an impatient tug.

"Lunch?" She stopped.

"For my family. To present my bride to them." He pulled her to him and linked his arms behind her back.

"Oh." She'd thought that once tonight was over she'd have Zac to herself. That from tomorrow they'd be alone. On their honeymoon, as he'd promised, without hordes of people and bodyguards. Obviously not. Enfolded in the circle of his arms, she still felt compelled to ask, "I thought we were going on honeymoon?"

"Afterward." He shot her a rakish smile, his face close to hers. "Be patient, wife. You haven't had a chance to meet my family—you told me that yourself. I've hogged you to myself for five whole days. But the whole clan are here—

it will be a while before they'll get together again. I thought
we'd take the opportunity to let you get to know them a little outside the crush of the wedding."

"I see." Instantly, she felt contrary, confused. She
wanted to be alone with Zac. But she also wanted to meet
his family, his best friends. She wanted to have a chance
to talk with Angelo and Tariq and get to know them better.
She wanted to ask Dimitri and Stacy what Zac had been
like as a little boy. And she wanted to meet his sister.

She wanted them to approve of her.

Zac was quite right. She should meet them. Tomorrow.
Nerves started to churn in her stomach. "What if they
don't like me?"

One hand came forward and tipped her chin up. "How
can they not? You're perfect." His teeth glittered in the
dim light, and she made out the glimmer of steel in his
eyes. "Who would dare question my judgement?"

Her stomach churned some more. Jeez, she was far from
perfect. Had Zac set her up on some sort of pedestal? She
licked suddenly dry lips. What if his sister hated her? Zac
would not tolerate anyone questioning his choice of bride.

Pandora bit her lip and told herself it would be okay. She
was the chosen bride of Zac Kyriakos. His family would
accept her or face the consequences. They would love her.

As Zac did.

They had to. She'd do her best to make it happen. And
what she couldn't get right, Zac would sort out. She
snuggled closer. Sometimes she forgot his power. Sometimes he was simply Zac, the man she adored.

"Stop worrying, everything will be okay." His head
dipped and his lips met hers. Pandora's breasts brushed his

chest and all her concerns vanished. All she could think of was Zac…his hungry mouth, the strength in the hard arms around her, holding her close, making every atom in her body vibrate with longing.

He tore his mouth away and drew a gasping breath of air. "Now can we leave?"

"Yes." She sighed.

Two

Zac strode to the drinks cabinet in the corner of the sitting room that formed part of the master suite and poured himself two fingers of the single malt scotch whisky he preferred. A couple of long, raking strides took him to the window. He stared blindly out, not seeing the city lights in the distance. All he could think about was the disturbing silence in his bedroom. His wife was on the other side of the door behind him. He wondered if she was ready for him.

His gut tightened.

He'd been waiting for this moment for three months. He'd been patient. A damned saint.

Throughout their courtship he hadn't dared stay in close proximity with his bride-to-be. He'd allowed himself only two fleeting visits, each flight on the Kyriakos Gulfstream jet taking twenty-five hours and necessitating a halfway stop in Los Angeles to refuel. The almost fifty hours he'd spent in the air had taken more time than he'd spent with his fiancée, but it had been worth it. To see her. To touch her.

Briefly.

Circumspectly.

And then he'd jetted off before he'd lost it. Before he pulled her into his arms, onto the wide bed in one of the luxurious wooden cabins he'd occupied at High Ridge Station and ravished her to the full extent of his need. His passion would have stunned her. It had shocked him.

Zeus, but she was temptation itself with her silky pale hair and wide-set silver eyes and her slight body with narrow wrists and ankles that made her look so delicate.

But now they were man and wife. All that separated them was a door. He swivelled and stared at the solid wooden door and swallowed.

He had to take it slowly, had to control the vast sea of desire that seethed inside him. The last thing he wanted was to terrify the wits out of his bride on her wedding night. Because Pandora was an innocent.

A virgin.

His virgin bride.

And now it was his wedding night.

Zac intended to savour every moment. Never in his thirty-one years had he made love to a virgin. His outdated sense of honour had always demanded that he choose women who knew the score as his lovers.

But his wife was a different matter.

He was horrified to discover he was nervous. His hands shook around the glass he held—and telling himself the nerves came from desire, not fear, didn't help. Zac stared into the amber liquid. He didn't drink as a rule. Had never been drunk in his life—nor even a little inebriated. He despised people who used their addictions as a crutch.

But tonight was different....

Tipping back his head, he downed the scotch and set the glass down. Plucking up his courage—Dutch courage, he thought mordantly—he made for the bedroom door.

Standing in the centre of Zac's rich burgundy-and-gold bedroom—her bedroom, too, now—and conscious of the immense bed behind her, Pandora watched as the heavy brass door handle twisted. Something squeezed tight deep inside her. The door opened and Zac stepped through.

He came to an abrupt standstill.

He'd showered, she saw at once, and changed his clothes. The close-fitting black pants and oversize white shirt were sexy as hell. She flushed as she realised he was watching her with as much interest as she assessed him. Instantly heat flickered in her belly and her breath caught in the back of her throat.

"You're still dressed." He sounded disappointed. "I thought I'd give you the chance to shower, to—"

"I need you to undo the buttons down the back," she rushed to speak. "I didn't think about arranging for anyone to be here to help me undo them." And no one had offered. Obviously the dressmaker who'd helped her get ready this morning had thought her bridegroom would relish the task. Just the thought made her flush. Quickly she continued, "I washed my face, but I need to get this gown off." She'd washed as well as she could, removed her makeup, brushed her teeth. Nothing more to do until the dress was gone.

"Of course! How stupid of me…I didn't think." He came nearer.

Excitement clamoured inside her. She tried not to shiver. But when he stood in front of her, the little tremors of anticipation started to race across her skin.

"Turn around," he whispered, dropping to his knees.

She needed no second bidding. The ancient silk rustled as she turned. She could hear Zac's steady breathing behind her, feel her heart start to pound as she waited….

A whisper of air caressed her ankles as he lifted the hem.

There was a small pull and she knew the lowest button was free. Little tug after little tug told her of Zac's successes as he worked his way up from the hem.

"*Zeus,* did the original seamstress have to use so many buttons? There must be at least two hundred—and they're tiny!"

"There are seventy-five buttons. The dressmaker doing the alterations counted them each time she took the dress off after a fitting. It takes forever to undo—even with a buttonhook."

"I dearly hope not." There was laughter in Zac's voice… and something else…something dark and sensual that caused her pulse to thrum through her head. "And I don't see a buttonhook."

She struggled to regain her composure. "If this were a fairy tale, you'd have waited one hundred years for this moment."

"I think I've been waiting my whole life," he muttered. Then he said, "If this were a fairy tale I wouldn't need a buttonhook. I'd have my magical trusted sword and I'd be able to slit a line down here—" His voice broke off and he traced a line from the small of her back, down over the curve of her bottom, and Pandora shuddered.

"Then I'd slide that dress off…." His voice trailed away, and she could hear that his breathing had speeded up.

"But you haven't got a magical sword, so you're going to have to do it—"

"The old-fashioned way. Slowly, taking my time, enjoying the experience," he murmured, and Pandora gasped as his hand slid up the inside of her calf, to her knee, where it stopped. "A couple more buttons and I'll be able to touch your thigh."

His fingers gave her bare skin a last caress, then slid away. Pandora sighed with disappointment.

"Don't worry, *yineka mou,* there will be lots of touching and stroking. We have the whole night ahead of us…and I'm going to take it very slowly. I promise."

"Then I think I might just die of pleasure tonight," she whispered, breathless from arousal.

"Aah, wife of mine, do not say such things. I am trying very hard to keep my cool. Don't melt it or it will all be over before we begin."

"I thought we'd already begun."

Zac groaned. "Wife, be silent! I need to undo these buttons as quickly as I can and you are distracting me." His breath caught and his hands stilled. "What the hell is this?"

"The garter. I wasn't sure if you followed the custom of throwing it…so I wore one anyway." Still kneeling behind her, his fingers moved again, soft against her thigh, running under the garter belt. "It's blue…for the rhyme. You know, *Something borrowed, something blue.* I thought the dress could pass as something borrowed." She was babbling now, but she didn't care. His touch was driving her crazy… and if she didn't babble, she might just grab that hand…

bring it around to her pebble-hard nipples for him to douse the aching.

But his fingers were retreating, and she could feel the garter sliding down her leg. He lifted her foot, hooked the garter off, then he spun her around, and rose to his full height.

She stopped breathing.

His face was taut, his eyes blazing, and he held the garter aloft like a trophy.

"Mine," he said hoarsely. "Every perfect bit of you is mine."

She didn't even have time to gasp before his lips landed on hers, hard and ravenous.

Stretching onto tiptoe, Pandora wrapped her arms around his neck, the impact of his chest against her rousing a wildness she'd never known, and she kissed him back as though she were starved, all the while pressing herself closer.

"Slowly, wife of mine, slowly," he panted, his big hands going to her hips, holding her off.

"I—"she punctuated it with a kiss "—can't—" another kiss "—wait."

"Ah, *Christos.*"

His hands cupped her buttocks, lifting her, the priceless dress ruching up around the tops of her thighs, pulling her close until…until…she could feel his hardness through the fabric. With a rough mutter he hoisted her higher, and her feet dangled off the ground. Zac lurched forward.

"*Zac!* You'll drop me." Hurriedly, she hooked her legs around his hips, her feet tangling with the soft silk folds of the dress as she clung on for dear life.

She landed on the bed with Zac sprawled on top of her. Breathlessly she stared up into hot green eyes.

"I can't wait—not another minute." His body moved against hers, restless and insistent.

She could feel his heat, his hardness, could sense that he was hanging on to his control by a fine thread. "The dress—we'll ruin it."

"Forget the dress!"

"I can't. The dressmaker kept eulogising about it being a piece of living history. I'd feel so guilty—"

"Shh. Roll over, then. Let me get the damned thing off," he growled and shrugged off his shirt.

In a brief second Pandora took in his naked chest gleaming in the soft golden light of the bedside lamps, the curve of his chest muscles, the lean tapered strength of his hard stomach and groaned.

And promptly nearly died of embarrassment.

Balling her fists against her mouth so that no more humiliating sounds would escape, she rolled onto her stomach so that he wouldn't see her face, wouldn't see the desire, the wanting…and then cringed as the skirts of the irreplaceable dress caught around her legs. "Oh, no."

"I'll set you loose." There was laughter in his voice now.

"It's not about me—"

"It's about the damned dress, I know." A hint of very real masculine frustration mingled with the humour.

How could she explain that she'd hate to be responsible for tearing or damaging a priceless heirloom?

Then she forgot all about the dress. Zac's hands had slipped through the slit he'd already unbuttoned, were on her skin. Smoothing, caressing.

"Nghh," she moaned. "I thought you were supposed to be undoing the buttons."

"This is much more fun, *agapi mou.*"

She leaped at the brush of his lips behind her knees. "Zac!"

He trailed a row of kisses along her tender, sensitised skin. Stopped. She waited, her heart pounding, tensing for what might happen next.

She heard a rustle of silk, felt the sleek, slick wetness of his tongue on the back of her smooth thigh. She gasped, then buried her mouth in the bed coverlet, willing herself to be silent, not to moan like a wanton.

He was pulling at the fabric caught under her. She lifted her hips. He tugged again and muttered something succinct in Greek.

"I am going to have to undo these buttons. Every damned one…without a buttonhook." He muttered an expletive, then laughed. "This time I'll start at the top. It will be easier on my restraint."

Thank God.

Pandora raised her face from the coverlet and rested her chin on folded arms. The breath whooshed out of her as his thighs straddled her and his weight settled astride her.

"Am I too heavy?"

"No."

His fingers brushed her nape and she went rigid.

"First button." There was resignation in his voice now. "Seventy-five, you said? And I doubt I've undone even half. *Ai mi!* How long is this going to take?"

"Perhaps we can make small talk?"

"Small talk?" He gave a snort of disgust.

Pandora bit back a smile. "Like, about the weather."

"Yes, let's talk about the weather. It's so hot that I can barely breathe, and tonight I'm even hotter, despite the air conditioner in here. Shall I describe exactly how hot I am?" He didn't wait for an answer. "My skin is so hot that it's tight."

At his harshly bitten out words Pandora had a searing visual of his chest just before she'd turned over and hidden her face. The sheen on the bronzed skin, the curve of his nude chest muscles. Jeez, she'd wanted to touch him. His skin would have been sleek and warm to her touch....

"What else?" she gasped.

"I am throbbing with something—a hunger—that I have never felt in my life before. I'm thirty-one years old and I feel like a damned boy. A boy who wants to grab... and squeeze...and possess. Hell, I'm not hot—I'm on goddamn fire."

Pandora couldn't think of a single thing to say in response to Zac's raw outburst. But she could feel. She could feel the rub of Zac's fingers as he loosed the tiny buttons, could feel the winnow of air against her naked skin as he peeled back the gown. She could hear the faint hum of the air-conditioning and his harsh breathing in the sudden silence of the vast bedroom.

"Okay, that's the weather taken care of. Any more small talk you fancy making?"

She stared blindly ahead, her body burning with arousal at the fierce onslaught of his erotic, highly charged words.

"Damn! I've shocked you, haven't I? Shocked you with the reality of my desires for you. Sometimes I forget how young and—"

"Zac—"

"—how innocent you are. All those years in a girls' boarding school, then helping your father, working in his business… I should be shot." He'd stopped fiddling with the buttons. "I told myself I'd take it slow, told myself I'd—"

"*Zac.*"

This time he heard her and broke off.

Unable to see his face, she drew a deep breath. This was difficult, more difficult than she'd ever anticipated. "I wasn't always at school or with my father. I visited with friends—"

"Your father told me," he interrupted. "Vacations with school friends, carefully vetted—that's hardly experience."

"I'm not a total innocent."

"What are you saying?" There was a fine shake of tension in the thighs clamped around her hips. She baulked. It was too late for this discussion, a discussion that she'd thought totally irrelevant in today's day and age. They were married, for goodness' sake. What difference would it make?

She put it all out of her mind and said throatily, "That I want you."

He gave a growl. His hands were back on the dress, tugging, fevered with impatience. "Damn these buttons! Pandora, my wife, I want you, too—more than I can tell you."

"So show me, don't tell me."

"I thought you wanted small talk." He gave a soft, husky laugh. "Perhaps we can talk about flesh…" He lifted more fabric from her back. "Or skin." A finger slid into the indent of her spine, along the length of the shallow groove. "Shall I tell you how soft your skin is?"

An exquisite sensation rippled down…down…pooling in her abdomen, sliding lower. Pandora shuddered and flexed her toes, anything to slow the pleasure that threatened to consume her. "Talk's cheap," she gurgled, struggling for air.

"So you want action?" And then his lips were *there* placing openmouthed kisses in the hollow of her spine. And his tongue…

Jeez, his tongue! She bit the back of her hand, determined not to let the moans escape. The maddening caresses eased. And she breathed again. The dress gave some more, his hands were working quickly now. Frenzied.

"At last."

She felt the cool air on her exposed buttocks as he peeled the fabric away, heard his gasp.

"*What is this?* Is it meant to drive me out of my skull with desire?" His voice was hoarse, his Greek accent pronounced. "Because, I swear to you, it's succeeding."

As his fingers hooked under the tiny bits of white Lycra that made up the minuscule thong she wore, the tremors started again. Stronger this time. Tremors that he must feel. She pictured what he saw: a Y made up of three laces of Lycra. Then there was the narrow triangle of delicate white lace in front that he couldn't see.

She struggled to find her voice. "That's the something new."

"What?" He sounded shell-shocked.

"*Something old, something new.* Remember? The rhyme I told you about? I thought the dress could do double duty and pass as something old as well as something borrowed."

"*Forget the dress.*" He tugged it out from under her, dropping it on the floor. "I don't want to hear another word about that damned old piece of silk. It's taken up far too much of our time this evening already." He stroked a long sweep down her back and whispered, "Your skin is living silk. Pandora, wife, you are amazing."

She didn't—couldn't—answer. A blast of desire unlike anything she'd experienced in her life shook her. Then his hands were running over the naked globes of her bottom, a finger tracing the white thread of the thong that laced across the small of her back. And he was kissing the depression at the base of her back. That finger—oh, glory, that finger—traced the last bit of thong down between her legs. She bit down harder in case she started to scream.

The yearning ache between her legs caused her to shift restlessly…she wanted him to touch her *there*.

"Is this what you want, *agapi?*"

His hand was under the whisper of white lace now, at the heart of her, his fingertips exploring the wet crease, touching the tight bud.

A moan broke from her.

She wriggled, opening her legs wider. Another stroke. She went rigid as sensation shafted through her.

"More?" he asked. And touched again.

She fought the ache…the desire…all the while craving—

"More," she panted.

This time he barely touched her, just the lightest teasing brush of his fingertips, and a fierce heat swept that tiny bead of flesh. This time she screamed and came apart in his arms. Then she lay there breathless, spent, feeling as if a firestorm has swept over her and heard Zac's murmur full of dark delight in her ear.

"There's much, much more to come. And we have all night long."

Three

"It is done."

Pandora tilted her head at the sound of Zac's beloved voice and paused in midstep on the balcony outside his study. She'd woken to find Zac gone, only a delicate long-stemmed white rose and a note on the pillow beside her. His writing was strong and slanted and told her that something had come up to which he needed to attend and he'd see her at breakfast in the sunroom downstairs.

She'd risen, placed the rose in a glass of water and picked the discarded wedding dress off the carpet and hung it up carefully. A quick shower to freshen up, and she'd pulled the first thing that came to hand—a filmy sundress with splashes of colour that clung in all the right places—out of the large walk-in cupboard where her clothes had been hung. Leaving her long hair loose, she sprayed a dash of fragrance behind her ears and came to find Zac, still dazed and glowing from the incredible lovemaking of the night before.

Her groom was not in the sunroom, so she skipped through the open doors onto the balcony where they'd kissed last night, wondering what people—his family, his friends, his colleagues—had made of their sudden disappearance from the reception.

Oh, jeez. She shut her eyes. They hadn't even stuck around long enough to cut the cake. Soon she'd have to face the knowing stares of Zac's family at lunch. She shuddered at the discomfiting idea.

The sound of voices halted her embarrassing thoughts. From where she lurked on the balcony she could see two men through the French doors—Zac and another man with his back to her. It was the other man who'd spoken. As he turned and raised a fluted glass, she recognised Dimitri, Zac's cousin. His best man. His best friend. And also his lawyer.

Dimitri had prepared the complex prenuptial contracts and been present when she and Zac had signed them three days ago. Initially she'd pushed aside her instinctive objection that legalities weren't necessary between her and Zac. But she'd known that Zac was a hardheaded businessman, known her father would expect them. A law firm in London which her father used had vetted them for her and suggested only minor changes.

She hadn't needed a prenuptial contract to feel secure. Zac's love had done that.

Embarrassed, she hesitated outside, uncertain what to do next. The last thing in the world she wanted was to walk into that room and meet Dimitri's gaze. Not after she and

Zac had departed so hurriedly last night. She wavered. She longed to wish Zac a good morning, kiss him and let him see the love and joy that bubbled inside her.

Through the crack in the curtains Zac looked utterly gorgeous. She stole another look as he clinked his glass with his cousin.

"I thought I'd never find her, Dimitri," Pandora heard him say. "My wedding is definitely cause to celebrate."

"*Vre,* you have been lucky. And so beautiful, too, you lucky dog."

Pandora grinned. Men! Love was not enough, beauty was always important. But she was touched at the relief in Zac's voice as he'd said *I thought I'd never find her.* His relief in finding someone to love.

She felt the same about him.

Yesterday he'd told her he thought she was perfect. Well, she disagreed. *He* was perfect. She was the luckiest—

"It is done—finally. Now there is no going back." Something about the tone of Zac's voice interrupted her musings and stopped her from rushing headlong into the room. She paid close attention. "No one knows better than you that this prophecy has been the bane of my life."

"I know, cousin. But it's tradition. A tradition that haunts the Kyriakos heir."

She listened harder, intrigued. What prophecy? What tradition? *What on earth were they talking about?*

Dimitri was still speaking. He'd crossed the room, his back to the glass doors. Pandora strained her ears to hear what he was saying. "It's the twenty-first century—you would've thought that the family, the public, would be prepared to let it go."

"They can't." Zac gave a harsh sigh. "And neither can I. The risks are too high."

"You mean, the likelihood of Kyriakos Shipping's share prices dipping are too high, don't you?"

"That, too."

Pandora cocked her head. What was all this about haunting and share prices? For an instant she considered pushing the door open, striding in and demanding an explanation. But something held her back. Something that filled her stomach with cold dread.

For a moment she considered turning, walking away, pretending she'd never heard whatever this conversation concerned. It scared her. Made her stomach cramp and apprehension swarm around inside her head like a clutch of bewildered bees.

Yes, she should pretend. She could retreat, then stamp her way back down the corridor, make an entrance that they would hear. She could look Dimitri straight in the eye and pretend that she and Zac hadn't rushed off to consummate their wedding vows with indecent haste. She could pretend that she'd never heard a thing about the prophecy that haunted Zac. *And then what?*

She'd never find out….

How could she ask later? How could she just drop it into conversation? *Oh, by the way, Zac, tell me about the prophecy. You know—the one that you thought would never be fulfilled?*

She'd married a man whose deepest secrets she didn't know.

No.

She wanted—needed—to hear more. Even if it was

not all good. After all, Zac loved her. She had nothing to fear. He'd married her very publicly. Made the love he felt for her clear to the world. The apprehension started to recede.

She was being silly letting the men's lowered voices build a terror of conspiracy within her.

When the footsteps came closer, Pandora shrank away from the door, panicking for an instant at what she would do if they found her standing out here, eavesdropping. Then she forced herself to get a grip. For goodness' sake, there was nothing ominous about what they were discussing.

If only this stupid, ridiculous chill in the pit of her stomach would go—

"To find a virgin, a beautiful virgin…my God, cousin, the odds were against you. But I envy you this morning."

A virgin? What did Dimitri mean *a virgin? They were talking about her.*

Then it hit her between the eyes. Jeez, she'd been so blind. This was the reason Zac had married her. Not because he loved her. Because he needed a virgin bride.

"That's my wife you're talking about, Dimitri. Be careful." The warning growl in Zac's tone did nothing to assuage the bile burning at the back of Pandora's throat.

She'd heard enough. No way could she walk in there and confront Zac and his cousin. Not about something as intimate as her virginity.

She ducked her head and wheeled around, walking faster and faster until she broke into a run.

The third door Pandora rattled was unlocked and opened into a bedroom. Pandora rushed in, pulled the door shut behind her and locked it before leaning her aching forehead against the hard door.

What was she to do?

"Can I help?"

The sweet voice came from behind her. Pandora straightened and spun around. The too-thin brunette in an ice-blue dress watching her with a questioning smile was a total stranger. Then the smile faltered and lines of concern etched into the other woman's forehead.

"Is everything all right?"

Pandora nodded jerkily. She wasn't ready to reveal what she'd learned to anyone, especially not a stranger. "I'm fine. Really."

Really, I'm not.

My world has just crashed down around my ears.

But she couldn't say that—she had a facade to maintain. A position as Zac Kyriakos's virgin bride. "I'm sorry…I've intruded," she said instead, and grimaced.

The brunette flapped a hand. "Don't worry about it. I'm Katerina—but most people call me Katy."

Katerina…*Katy.*

Pandora stared into familiar green eyes, warmer for sure but still the same hue. "You're Zac's sister."

"Yes. And you're Zac's wife." The bright smile was back. "You're beautiful. My brother has fabulous taste. And I know he's never going to forgive me for missing the wedding—" Katy's smile wavered "—but I hope you will. I've been dying to meet you. I only arrived in Athens this morning."

"Of course I'll forgive you." Pandora noticed the faint dimple beside the woman's mouth—just like Zac's. "And I'm sure Zac will, too."

"Maybe." The dimple deepened. "You're lucky, Pandora. I tell you, he's the best brother in the entire world. I hope we'll be friends."

Pandora instantly liked this warm woman. "Of course we'll be friends."

"Great!" Katy extracted a tube of lipstick from a small sequined bag, popped off the lid and ran it over her lips. "That's better." She eyed her reflection in the mirror. "My husband never understands why us women always want to look perfect all the time." She threw Pandora a wicked, laughing look. "He insists on kissing it all off."

"Is he here?" Pandora glanced around but saw nothing to evidence masculine occupation. Zac had said that Katy's husband was a difficult man to be married to. Had he not wanted Katy to attend Zac's wedding? Greek families were so close that would certainly add tension.

"I wish he was." Katy sounded wistful.

Was the problem between Katy and her husband? Or did the real source of tension lie between her brother and her husband? Pandora couldn't help wondering if Katy was caught between two dominant Greek men—the juicy bone between two alpha dogs. Katy clearly adored her brother and it was obvious she missed her absent husband.

Katy was fortunate. She was loved. For a moment Pandora felt envy blossom inside her, green and ugly. She thrust the unwelcome emotion away and ruthlessly suppressed a pang of self-pity.

"I'll call you in a week or so, we can meet for lunch," Katy was saying.

Pandora nodded. Her heart lifted. The lost feeling started to recede. "That will be lovely."

Katy patted her hand. "You looked so unhappy when you came in—don't let anyone spoil what you and my brother have."

Instantly reality came crashing back. What did they have? At worst, a sham of a marriage based on a pack of lies. At best, it was an illusion built on her naive assumption that Zac loved her.

What good would running do? She needed to find Zac. To get to the bottom of what she'd heard. To find out whether he'd married her because he loved her or because he needed a convenient virgin bride.

"No," Pandora said slowly. "I won't let anyone spoil what we have." But she couldn't help thinking it had been spoiled…ruined…already. By Zac's Academy Award-deserving deception.

The study was empty. Pandora found Zac in the elegant sitting room, reclining in the leather armchair positioned under the Chagall painting she'd admired when she'd first seen this room. With one knee crossed over the other, Zac perused the morning paper. Her heart started to thump.

"I need to talk to you."

He glanced up and a lazy, intimate smile softened his strong features. "Good morning, wife."

"Is it? A good morning?" She raised her brows and gave him a pointed little smile.

His mouth curved wider until white teeth flashed irresistibly against his tanned olive skin. Masculine satisfaction gleamed in his eyes. "You tell me."

"I'm not so sure."

"You're not sure? Come here, I'll show you. Last

night…" His voice trailed away as he leaned over and caught her behind the knees and swept her onto his lap. "Last night didn't convince you? I'll have to do something about that."

In his arms, Pandora turned to marshmallow. The sexy, suggestive timbre of his voice in her ear, the hard-muscled chest pressing against her side were almost enough to convince her to abandon the answers she sought. Almost.

"You are so beautiful." He pressed a kiss against her cheek and hugged her closer. "A good-morning kiss will have to do for now. We don't have enough time to make it to the bedroom, not with my family due to arrive any minute for lunch. Come closer, let me adore you with my lips, let me—"

"Stop it, Zac!" She turned her head away just before his lips landed on her mouth. "There's no need for such reverence."

He stilled. "What do you mean?"

She sat straight, no easy feat given that she sprawled across his lap, her colourful sundress bunched around his legs. "I know, Zac."

His eyes suddenly wary, he asked. "What do you know?"

Gauging his response, she peered at him from behind her fringe. "I know *everything*."

"Everything?"

"I know about the prophecy, about your need to marry a virgin bride."

"And?" He prompted, his astute eyes suddenly hooded. "What else do you know? Surely that can't be all."

She took a deep breath. "I know you don't love me."

He flicked her a quick upward glance. "And why do you think that?"

"Because you never told me. And I never realized…"

"But I—"

"Let me finish." She brushed her bangs back and glared at him. "You did such a great job of it that I never even realized you'd never told me you loved me. Jeez, I've been stupid."

"I told you—"

"Yes, let's revisit exactly what you told me. *You're so beautiful, Pandora. I love your hair. The pale gold reminds me of*—"

"Sea sand." Zac stretched out a hand and brushed the strands away from her face. "It does. It's so soft, so pale."

Pandora pushed his caressing hand away and stood. "Then what about *I love your energy—like quicksilver,* huh?"

"You never stop moving, it's intriguing. Your hands are so small, so fine-boned, yet they move so swiftly, even when you talk. Even now when you're mad."

She clenched her fists and put them behind her back. "And you love my laughter, too, huh?"

He nodded slowly, his eyes watchful. "A sense of humour is important in a marriage."

"And then there was *I love the way you make me feel.*"

"Definitely."

"But you know what? You never said *I love you, Pandora.* And given all these things you told me, I never thought anything of it." *Until now.* "It never crossed my mind that it was a clever way of getting out of—"

"Hey, wait a moment…" Zac straightened and pushed his hands through his hair. She'd never seen him look anything but coolly and good-humouredly in control. Now his hair stood up in all directions and a frown snaked across his forehead as he perched on the edge of the armchair.

"So say it, Zac."

He looked at her in disbelief. "You're kidding me, right?"

"I'm not kidding. I'm waiting, Zac."

He gave a short, unamused laugh and shrugged. "This is about three little words?"

"I overheard you talking. I heard that you need to marry a virgin. Right now I need those three little words."

"What the hell do they matter?" He stood, towering over her. "We're married. We're compatible. *On every level.* Do you know how rare that is? You understand my world—something that's very important to me. We share interests, a sense of humour. And as for sex…well—" he blew out "—that's better than I ever hoped for."

"Lucky you! Because I feel like I've been cheated." At her angry words, his head went back and his eyes flashed. "So when were you planning to tell me, Zac?"

His gaze dropped away.

"You weren't, were you? You were planning to let me live in the clouds, to think this was the love match of the century." She turned away, not wanting him to see what the realisation had cost her.

"Wait—"

"Wait?" She gave an angry laugh and spun to face him. "*Why?* For you to make a fool of me all over again?"

Zac stared into her furious countenance. Underneath the tight-lipped anger he thought he caught a glimpse of hurt in her stunning pale eyes. Those eyes that had held him entranced since the first moment he'd seen her.

She wanted him to say that he loved her.

He gulped in air. *God, what was he to do?*

"My family will be here soon. Let's discuss this later." And saw instantly it had been the wrong thing to say. Her fury grew until her eyes glimmered an angry incandescent silver.

"*Your family?* What do I care about your family? I've hardly even met them! For almost a week I've been trying to get you to introduce me to them. Every time you put me off. Stupid me, I was flattered. Thought it meant you wanted to spend all your free time alone with me. But I was deluding myself, wasn't I? You just didn't want me to meet them in case someone let slip that you needed to marry a virgin."

"It wasn't like that," he replied lamely.

"So what was it like? Explain to me, Zac. In little one-syllable words that even a fool like me can understand. Or are you incapable of using those one-syllable words like *I love you?*"

Zac blinked at the unexpected attack. "You're not a fool—"

"Oh, please! Don't give me that. You've played me like a master. Convinced me you loved me. Jeez, I can't believe how naive I've been. Why would you fall for me, a—"

"Because you're young, beautiful and—"

"And a stupid, pretty little virgin?" She gave him a tight smile. When he failed to respond, she added, "So what if I'm young and beautiful. What do appearances matter anyway? It doesn't say anything about the person I am inside. Good. Terrible. Or didn't you care as long as I was a pretty stupid little virgin?"

The urge to laugh in appreciation at the clever way she'd twisted her own words rose in him, but one glance at her face convinced him that she would not appreciate it. "Pandora." He took her hand. "I wasn't—"

The door swung open. "Zac, people are starting to arrive," Katy said anxiously, then put her hand over her mouth as she took in their obviously confrontational stances. "I'm out of here. But, brother, you need to get to the crowd downstairs."

"Katy, I want to introduce you to—"

But Katy was already gone.

"Don't worry, I introduced myself to your sister all by myself. Tell me, does she also know I'm a virgin?"

Zac took a deep breath and forced himself to ignore the inflammatory remark. "My family is here. I don't want them embarrassed. Humour me. I need you to pretend everything is fine between us. Please?"

"Pretend? You mean, like you *pretended* you loved me?"

Zac winced as her bitter words hit home. "My family mean a lot to me. I don't want them to see this discord between us—not when we only exchanged vows yesterday. We can talk it all out later, I promise you."

"Later?" She gave him a searing look of suspicion. "When?"

"As soon as my family are gone. Act out the charade for two hours, that's all I ask."

"Two hours?" Zac held his breath as she gave him a killing look. "Fine! I'll *pretend* for two hours and then we talk."

He let out a silent sigh of relief. "Thank you. You won't regret it."

"I hope not." There was a fevered glitter in Pandora's eyes that stirred remorse in him. Hurt sparkled in the clear depths—or were those tears? Hell, he'd *never* intended for her to find out.

Lunch was finally over. Pandora glared at the five-tier wedding cake, her fingers clenched around a large silver knife. Zac's hand, large and warm, rested over hers.

"Your hands are cold," he murmured in her ear.

Her hands? What about her heart? It thudded painfully, cold and bleak in her tight chest. Just thinking about Zac's betrayal made her poor heart splinter into tiny, painful little pieces. Zac didn't love her—had never loved her—had only married her because he thought her a perfect little virgin.

Perfect.

God, how she hated that word. How—

"Make a wish," Zac whispered, his breath curling into her ear. The familiar frisson of desire ran down her spine. His hand tightened around hers and pressed down.

Please, God, let this mess sort itself out, she prayed, and the knife sank through the pristine white wedding cake.

"Later I'll tell you what I wished for," Zac's voice was warm and husky against her ear.

Later? Jeez, but he was arrogant! He sounded so sincere, so loving. And there would be no later for them. Not anymore.

Pandora half wished she could go back to that blissful state of ignorance, before she'd learned the truth. Instead of this emptiness that filled her now. But what use would that be? She'd only be kidding herself. *Pretend,* Zac had said, and that's exactly what she was doing.

"Smile," his voice crept into her thoughts, and a second later a burst of silver-white light exploded in her face.

She looked wildly around at the throng, the people.

Katy grinned at her from behind an oversize camera. Pandora struggled to smile back.

No, this was not her life. *This public pretence.* The glimpse of what her life married to Zac would be like was devastatingly sad. Nothing more than a series of hollow pretences for public show from one day to the next—if she stayed. But she didn't have to stay trapped in a marriage to a man who wanted her only because she was a virgin.

Pretend?

Never. Zac was about to discover the extent of the error he'd made.

"Good, you are packed."

Pandora glanced to where Zac loomed in the doorway, immaculate in a lightweight suit over a white T-shirt worn with fashionable European aplomb. "I'm leaving, Zac. The fairy tale is over." She hefted a suitcase off the bed. "I think it would be best for all concerned if this marriage was annulled."

"Annulled?" Zac stared at her. "*Annulled?* This marriage can never be annulled. It's already been consummated."

Pandora raised her chin a notch. "Then I want a divorce. I'm not staying in a marriage with a man who doesn't love me."

A shadow moved across his face. "Pandora—"

She took a step toward the door…toward him. "No, I gave you the two hours of *pretend* you wanted. You're not going to sweet-talk me out of this—"

"There can be no divorce."

Stopping short of the threshold, she looked up at him. "What do you mean there can be no divorce? You're not the man I married. That man would never have pretended to love me. I want a divorce."

His face hardened. But instead of taking issue with her challenge, he spoke to the man behind him. "Take the bags, Aki."

"Hey, wait a minute. Those are my bags and my—"

"You said you were going. Aki will take your bags downstairs for you."

Was that all he was going to say? Pandora stared into his inscrutable face. Hard. Distant. A world apart from the man she'd married. Her mouth moved, but no words came out. She swallowed.

Was it over so easily?

She'd expected some resistance. A challenge. A huge wave of disappointment rocked her. Aki hoisted up her bags and headed down the stairs. Turning away from Zac, she moved back into the room and crossed to the dressing table to pick up the rainbow-hued silk scarf and designer handbag she'd so nearly left behind with all the turmoil stewing inside her. A quick check inside the bag revealed her wallet, her cell phone and her passport.

She tried not to let her shoulders sag. There was a thick knot at the back of her throat, but she wasn't going to let Zac see her cry.

The last thing she wanted was for him to know how much she cared—how much she'd loved him. How much his silent surrender to her demand for a divorce had devastated her. Fiercely she said, "I need to call the airport to book a seat."

There was a pause. Then Zac said, "Everything is being taken care of."

"Already?" She spun around to find him right behind her.

"I'll take you to the airport if that's what you want." His hand touched her elbow. "But first we talk. Alone, without interruption."

"We can talk on the way to the airport." She shrugged his hand off and glanced around the immense bedroom—the room where he'd made such devastating love to her and taught her about the power of being a woman. Stuff she'd never known.

Last night…no, she wasn't thinking about last night. About the tender passionate lover whom she'd *stupidly* believed loved her with all his heart.

With a jerky movement Pandora swung on her heel and made for the door. She charged through the sitting room in a blur of tears. Furiously she blinked them back.

Downstairs there was nobody to be seen. A sense of desolation overtook her. No one in the huge mansion cared that she was going, no one cared enough to say goodbye. She thought of asking to see Katy, then shook the thought away. What did it matter? She'd never see Zac's sister again.

Outside, the paved sweep of drive was empty. No one strolled in the parklike grounds, Mount Pendeli rising up in a solid mass of green beyond.

The only person to be seen was Aki crossing the driveway as he made his way to a circle of concrete set on the edge of the grassy park, where he deposited her bags.

"Where's the taxi?" She glared accusingly at Zac.

"*Christos.* Do you really think I'd see my wife off by taxi—like some common…" He paused, but she got the message. And then he reached out and grabbed her hand. "Come."

Almost running to keep up with his long, brisk stride,

she crossed the drive and then she was back on the grass. The sun blazed in the halcyon sky overhead. Pandora's heels sank into the perfectly manicured lawn. Aki had disappeared. Ahead lay the flat circle of concrete. A row of cypress trees lined the drive that led to the large electronic gates in the distance. Why had she not noticed how much those gates resembled prison bars before?

Surely he didn't mean to dump her outside the gates of his property? No, Zac would not do that to her. She was certain of that. He'd said he wanted to talk, so where was he taking her? She dug in her heels, dragging him to a stop. "Where are we going?"

"I'm taking you away. Where we can be alone, where we can sort this—this *misunderstanding*—out."

"Oh, no. I'm going to the airport. There's plenty of time to talk on the way."

"You're my wife, I am—" A deafening drone drowned out the rest of his reply. He grabbed her arm. Pandora resisted, determined not to let Zac dictate to her. Through the roaring noise she was aware that Zac was shouting at her.

She glared at him. "What?"

"Get down! Get back!" he yelled close to her ear.

The huge black shadow of a helicopter swept over them. Shuddering, finally comprehending, she let him pull her out of the path of the hovering machine.

Aki had returned with another batch of bags. These must belong to Zac, Pandora realised as the helicopter settled onto the concrete helipad and Aki started passing the bags—hers, too—up into the belly of the helicopter.

Zac's bags and her bags being loaded into the helicopter did not equate to her plan of going to the airport. She stared at the monstrous machine, its shiny white body bearing the royal-blue-and-yellow logo of Kyriakos Shipping. For the first time she saw the stylised feminine profile with long flying hair within the logo for what it was. A virgin. Then the slowing rotor blades grabbed her attention.

Pandora's stomach clenched and a fine attack of perspiration broke out along the back of her neck. "I'm not going anywhere with you. Especially not in that—" she stabbed a finger at the helicopter "—hellishly dangerous thing. I want a taxi to the airport. I'm leaving. I want a divorce."

"That's not going to happen."

Zac's bronzed face was hard. Inscrutable. This was not the man she'd fallen in love with. This was someone else altogether. A stranger, stripped of the indulgent, cherishing mask. A man so hard she feared he'd break her.

As he'd already broken her heart.

"How could I ever have agreed to marry you? I *hate* you."

Something moved across his face, a flash of darkness, and then it was gone. "That's too bad. Because we're going on honeymoon, to be alone—like you wanted."

"No way!"

There was a reckless gleam in his eyes. "Well, then, what have I got to lose?"

Picking her up, he hoisted her over his shoulder and tore across the grass to the open doors of the helicopter.

"No," she yelled, fear making her stiff.

He ignored her.

Each stride he took caused her to lurch against his shoulder, and with one hand she clung to her handbag while the other clutched his shirt.

"Put me down!" Pandora caught a glimpse of Aki's

startled face as Zac clambered into the helicopter, his arms tight as chains around her.

"Stop fighting me."

"Never," she vowed as she tumbled down onto his lap, her hair plastered to her face as tears clogged her eyes.

Zac shouted something at the pilot. The helicopter started to rise. Pandora hammered her fists against Zac's chest. "Let me out!"

She pushed back her streaming hair. In a blur of horror she stared out the window. Below, Zac's huge house was retreating, growing smaller. She let out a wail of disbelief, of sheer terror.

"Hush, you are making a scene."

Pandora realised she was sobbing. "That's all you can say? You kidnap me, then tell me to be quiet?"

"You're crying." His hand smoothed her hair.

"Of course I'm crying." She twisted her head away from his touch. "I don't believe you! Who the hell do you think you are?"

But she knew. He was Zac Kyriakos. One of the richest men in the world. So powerful that he could do what he liked with her. No one would stand in his way.

Four

When the descent started, Pandora lifted her face out of her hands and glimpsed the dark bronze disc of the sun glowing in the western sky against a fiery display of clouds. Out of the window she watched the darkening ground rushing up beneath the helicopter with a sense of frozen horror.

They were going to crash.

She was going to die. Panic bit into her and she struggled not to scream, knowing once she started she'd never stop.

Her fingers twisted around the soft, colourful scarf she'd rescued from her handbag and clung to like a talisman during the flight. She closed her eyes, hating the helplessness. And tried not to think about it. Not about what was happening to her now. And certainly not about the twisted metal wreck that burned in her darkest nightmares.

At last the helicopter rocked and settled on the ground.

A wave of uncontrollable anger swept her. How *dared* Zac do this to her?

Grabbing her handbag, she stormed to the door. The instant the pilot opened the door, she shot out, her legs almost collapsing under her as they met solid ground.

"Slow down." Zac was at her side, his hand under her elbow. She shrugged it off.

"Don't touch me," she snapped at him.

"You could've fallen."

"I would rather fall than have you touch me." Head bent to avoid the slowing rotor blades, she didn't look back as she scurried away. Once safe from the blades, she straightened. The rough fingers of the evening sea wind tugged her hair and the strands whipped across her eyes.

"That's not what you were saying last night. Then it was *Oh, Zac. Yes, Zac!* Last night you couldn't get enough of my touch."

At the taunting whisper, she turned and glared, brushing the hair out of her face with an impatient hand.

In the dusky light she could see the strange smile twisting his face, adding a cynical edge that caused her temper to flare higher.

"That was last night," she bit out. "Before I discovered that you'd misled me. Used me. I hate you, you know that? I've never said that to anyone in my life before. But I mean it—I really, *really* hate you."

The caustic, knowing smile vanished. For a second, stark shock flared in his eyes and he looked shaken by her response. A shadow fell across his face and all emotion leached out, leaving his gloriously sensual features hard and cold.

"Get a hold of yourself, Pandora. You're starting to sound hysterical."

The icy tone shook her. He spun away, and to her consternation Pandora watched as he strode across the flat rooftop, his suit jacket flapping in the wind. Anguish twisted inside her. How had it come to this? What had happened to the affinity, the sense of rightness between her and Zac?

Had he ever cared about her?

Or had it all been an elaborate charade?

Before they'd left Athens he'd said he was taking her somewhere they could talk. A quick look around the castellated parapets, sheer, steep white walls that ended on a slab of black rocks licked by the lazy sea far below revealed this was not quite the kind of venue she'd had in mind. Jeez, not even Rapunzel would've gotten out of here. *Where on earth were they?*

All she knew was that this godforsaken place was where Zac intended to have their showdown. She set her jaw and vowed not to let him walk all over her. She had some stuff to say to him, too. Her stomach turned over just thinking about that. But what choice did she have? Straight talk was all that was left.

And then she'd be off home to New Zealand on the very next flight. And Zac Kyriakos, his handsome face, gorgeous body and immense wealth could go to hell. She wasn't staying married to a man who didn't love her.

Ahead, Zac disappeared through an arch into the castle. Or eyrie. Or whatever this whitewashed structure was. Pandora was annoyed to find herself scurrying in his wake. She paused in the shadows at the top of a set of stone stairs that spiralled down into the heart of some kind of tower where wall sconces lit the whitewashed walls. Zac was already two levels down, his footfalls ringing against the hard stone.

"What about my luggage?" she called down.

"Georgios will attend to it," Zac tossed over his shoulder without slowing his pace.

"I hate you."

The staccato beat of his shoes against the stairs drummed the horrible words into a crazy kind of rhythm inside Zac's head and left him reeling.

I hate you. *I hate you.* The echo grew louder and louder until he wanted to bang his forehead against the curving walls of the tower that surrounded him and watch the stone to crumble into dust…the way his dreams had.

But he couldn't. He was Zac Kyriakos. That kind of behaviour did not become him. So he squared his shoulders like the man he was, the man he'd been born and raised to be, and tried to convince himself that it wasn't relief that coursed through him when at last Pandora's footfalls sounded on the stone stair treads far above.

Good, she was following.

He slowed his pace a fraction. There'd been a moment after they'd disembarked from the helicopter when he'd wondered if she would. But she'd given in. He told himself that he'd never expected any other outcome, never doubted she would do exactly as he wanted.

Even though she hated him.

Zac was waiting when Pandora finally exited the stairwell onto a wide terra-cotta-tiled landing that branched off to a narrow kitchen on one side and a huge sitting area to the other. Pandora caught a glimpse of stainless steel and pale marble bench tops in the unexpectedly modern galley-style kitchen before Zac gestured her forward.

"This way." He spoke in a cold, distant tone, and nerves balled her stomach in a tight knot.

She followed him into a large, airy space—and gasped at the sight of the sunset-streaked sky. Glassed on three sides, the space gave an impression of height and light and freedom, of seeing the world from the perspective of a gull in the sky. A rapid scan of her surroundings revealed a pair of long ivory leather couches separated by a heavy bleached-wood coffee table. An immense cream flokati rug added softness to the room without breaking the mono-chromatic colour scheme. Like the stairwell, the walls in here were covered with rough plaster and washed with white. And nothing detracted from the incredible impact of the sky and sea turned gold by the setting sun.

Except the brooding man standing an arm's length from her.

Pandora gave him a quick glance and looked away, a frown pleating her brow. So he was affronted because she didn't want him near her? Because she'd lashed out that she hated him? What the hell did he expect given the way he'd behaved?

Kidnapping her.

Thrusting her into that flying monster.

Agitated, she brushed back the tendrils of hair that the buffeting wind on the rooftop had tousled. "You know, I haven't been up in a helicopter for years." Her voice shook with a mixture of anguish and rage and long-suppressed emotion.

He swivelled on his heel, arrogance in every line of that

hard, lean body, and balled his hands on his hips, watching her from behind inscrutable eyes. "I really don't care about the last time you went joyriding."

"God, I hate you!"

Pandora itched to smack that insolent, cold-as-marble mask. But her hands were trembling so much she doubted she would succeed. Where had she ever gotten the idea that his eyes were tender, loving? That the hard slash of his mouth revealed passion and humour? That this stranger *loved* her?

The urge for straight talk that had raised its head less than ten minutes ago vanished. He didn't deserve any explanation of her terror. He didn't deserve to hear about… about…about the other stuff she needed to tell him. His thuggish behaviour, his lack of consideration for her, had put him beyond the pale. She didn't owe him a thing. He could take his talk and stick it where it hurt most—she wasn't staying around.

Reaching for her handbag, Pandora struggled to unzip it. Her shaking fingers groped and encountered the smooth cover of her cell phone. She pulled the phone out, clutching it like a lifeline.

"I'm going to phone my father and then this nonsense is going to stop. He'll send someone to come fetch me."

Zac's gaze dropped to the phone in her hand. "There's no reception on the island."

"The island? *We're on an island?*" Pandora's voice rose until she could hear the shrill tinge of hysteria he'd mentioned so scathingly.

"Yes, Kiranos. My hideaway. Only my close family knows of its existence. It's where I come to unwind. No phones, no bodyguards—only the simple pleasures in life."

The gaze that rested on her face was filled with grim contemplation. "Just peace and quiet."

"I don't believe that!" She swept a quick look around and then out over the expanse of sea. And swallowed. "You're far too important to put yourself out of reach." Pandora hated the sliver of doubt that crept into her voice as she considered that this unknown Zac might well have set up this godforsaken place to be out of touch with the rest of the world.

"Believe it. Cell phones are useless on Kiranos."

Kiranos…an island. She struggled to come to terms with his unwelcome revelation. He'd brought her here to talk and be alone. Realisation dawned. He'd never intended to have a brief conversation and take her to the airport.

An island. Bang went her plan of getting on the next flight…unless she wanted to swim for it. Her gaze swept the vista ahead of her. No other landmasses. No ships.

A few quick steps took her to the wall of glass that translated into a set of sliding doors. Another step, and she stood on a narrow, windy deck suspended high above the rocky beach below. She stared over the glass balustrade at the endless stretch of water that gleamed like liquid gold far below. No, she'd never make the distance across the sea. She was trapped. Trapped with the formidable stranger who was her husband.

The only way she was going to get off this piece of rock with its moat of seawater was to convince him to release her. To *talk*—oh, God, that word again—her way out of it.

And she had to succeed.

With an impatient huff, she flipped the cover of the cell phone shut and stepped back inside to where Zac waited, unsmiling.

"So what am I supposed to do here?"

"Relax. Sunbathe. Gaze at your navel." He glanced at her from under those impossibly long lashes and added softly, "Make love…."

She flinched and dropped the phone. It thudded onto the floor. Zac bent to scoop it up.

Putting her hands on her hips, she faced him down. "You're mad, you know that? Totally psycho. You kidnap me, put me in a helicopter…now you expect me to make love? I hate—"

"You hate me. I know, I know. That refrain is becoming a bore." But a muscle worked in his cheek.

Emotion choked her, a painful knot in her throat. "You know nothing. But you think you know it all." To her horror, she felt the tightness of tears at the back of her throat. "Why, Zac? Why did you marry me? Obviously not because you loved me! Why did you bring me here with a drummed-up excuse that you wanted to talk? *Why can't you let me go?* What's so special about a virgin in this day and age, for goodness' sake?"

He stared at her, his eyes empty holes in that hard face.

Another swallow to ease the sudden dryness in her mouth. So perhaps it would be better to start the talk thing he'd been so hot on sooner rather than later. She didn't care for this silent, inscrutable Zac.

She tried another tack. "Tell me about this prophecy you and Dimitri were talking about. I deserve to know, don't you think?"

"Okay." Zac sighed and rubbed a hand over his face. His shoulders sagged and suddenly he looked so weary, so disillusioned, that Pandora was tempted to rush to him, throw her arms around him and comfort him. Then she came to her senses. Why on earth was she feeling sorry for him?

This was Zac.

Zac who'd laughed with her, hugged her and pretended to love her. Zac who'd lied to her. Zac whom she'd married yesterday in the wedding of the decade, promising never to forsake. Zac who'd brought her to this rock with a castle on it to *talk* to her. Well, now he could damn well talk.

"Go on," she invited with a barbed little smile.

He ignored the taunt.

"Let me get us something to drink." Moments later he was back with two short, squat glasses filled with blocks of ice and mineral water. He set them down on the wooden coffee table and shrugged off his jacket.

Pandora couldn't help noticing how the white T-shirt clung to his broad shoulders. Quickly she averted her gaze, picked up her glass and took a long sip. "You were going to tell me about this prophecy," she reminded.

He inclined his head. "It's a legend rather than a prophecy. Sit down, it will take time."

Pandora sank down onto the leather sofa and Zac settled himself opposite her. "I told you that my great-grandfather repaired the family fortunes after the first World War?"

Pandora nodded, her interest caught despite her resolve not to be sucked in by his explanations. "Orestes Kyriakos married a wealthy Russian princess and used some of her funds to rebuild the Kyriakos Shipping fleet."

"That's right. After the Suez Canal was opened, Orestes followed in the footsteps of Aristotle Onassis and Stavros Niarchos and built his first supertanker to transport crude oil. When my grandfather, Socrates, took over Kyriakos Shipping, he continued to commission more supertankers. And by the time the oil crisis hit in the early seventies, Socrates had gone into the production of crude oil. He established three refineries and he left those to my cousin, Tariq, whose mother—my aunt—married the Emir of Zayed."

"I didn't realise that."

"Socrates's remaining grandson, Angelo, inherited three islands and a string of resorts that Socrates owned." He paused. "But I digress. My father lacked the magic Kyriakos touch—he lost more money than he ever managed to make. My grandfather called him an idle playboy and took me out of his care when I was six years old. Said he didn't want my father's sloth rubbing off on me. He considered my father a disgrace to the Kyriakos name and disinherited him in his will. He raised me, didn't want me to be the failure my father was."

"Didn't your mother object when he took you away?"

Zac glanced at her sideways. "My mother had an addictive personality. She was in and out of rehab—she had enough alcohol problems without worrying about me. She was hardly more than a child when she married my father at seventeen and fell pregnant with me soon after."

Pandora's heart went out to the little boy he'd once been. But when she started to say something, Zac interrupted, "With the exception of my father, the Kyriakos men have always been associated with wealth and acumen. And beautiful women." He shot her a hooded look and Pandora bit back her instant derogatory response. "Orestes was rumoured to have rescued his princess from the Bolshevik revolution, although there were some who said he stole her from her father—she brought a fortune in jewels as her dowry."

"She was beautiful." Pandora had seen the painting that hung in the entrance hall to Zac's house.

"Before that there was an English heiress and a shah's daughter, as well as—"

"And were all these beautiful paragons virgins?" Pandora interrupted.

Zac gave her a long look. "Yes. It was their innocence that initially attracted a Kyriakos male and their purity of spirit that kept him faithful all the years of their marriage."

"Oh, please."

"It's true," he insisted. "Kyriakos men do not stray from the marriage bed."

"What about your playboy father?"

"He was an aberration. A disgrace to the Kyriakos name and my grandfather disowned him. But even my father never dared divorce my mother and he failed to live up to the family name. There is no divorce. Ever. The sacredness of the marriage lies at the heart of the prophecy. A woman pure of body and spirit means a faithful man, sufficient heirs and wealth forever."

"You believe all this?"

His eyes flickered. "It doesn't matter whether I believe it. It's the legend. It is what is expected. It's a self-fulfilling prophecy that no Kyriakos heir worthy of the name has seen fit to disturb for nearly a thousand years since the Fourth Crusade. That was when the first documentation appeared about the legend—in the journal of an ancestor who rescued the daughter of a silk merchant, a woman who was reputed to be as innocent as a lamb, more beautiful than Helen of Troy and more wealthy than Croesus."

"What happened to your ancestor during the Fourth Crusade?" Despite herself, Pandora's interest was tagged.

"He came to live in Athens—on the same piece of land where my home stands. Byzantium did not take part in the crusades. There were issues with Rome." Zac's jaw was tight. "War is a cynical business, and the lure of instant wealth in Byzantium caused a few of the Venetian nobleman to end their crusade long before they reached Syria. The pickings were easy, the people less fierce and the rewards didn't mean facing an army. My ancestor saved the young woman from a marauding Venetian knight who treated her as little more than a slave—her only use to him was for ransom."

"So your ancestor stole her for her maidenhead and her wealth. What makes you think she grew to love him?"

"When he settled in Athens—a village then compared to Constantinople—he built her a castle. And beside the castle had a church erected. The castle no longer exists, but the church that he built for her in 1205, according to the family journal, still stands. It's now a national monument. And an inscription in the church records their love for each other."

Infuriated, Pandora cut across him. "And because your Kyriakos ancestors abducted their brides you think that gives you justification to kidnap me? Guess what? You're dead wrong about that. You had no right—"

"Pandora…" He moved to sit on the couch beside her. "You're right. This is not about my ancestors. We need to talk about us."

She froze as he came closer. Shaking her head so that her pale, long hair flew around her face, she said, "No, I don't want to talk about us. And it *is* about who you are, where you come from."

"Hell." He raked a hand through his hair and leaned back. "You make me sound like an alien from another universe."

"Perhaps you are." Annoyed and frustrated, she frowned at him. "I need to understand why a modern man gives credence to ancient superstition and waits years to find a virgin bride."

"I would never have married you if you weren't also—"

"Tell me one thing, Zac," Pandora interrupted him as she perched on the edge of the sofa, tension humming through her as she scanned his features. "Would I ever have merited a second look if I hadn't been a virgin?"

There was silence. "No." His reply was subdued. "I heard about this heiress who lived at the end of the world who was beautiful and innocent and I hoped—"

"That's why you came down to New Zealand instead of sending a minion? Not to see my father to broker some business deal?" Pandora could hear her voice rising again and she forced herself to speak calmly. "To look me over?"

Another hesitation. "I came to meet you, to get to know you."

"Oh, God!"

"But I would never have taken it to the next level, asked you to marry me, if I hadn't been sure—"

"I can't believe this!" Pandora threw her hands into the air. "It's the twenty-first century. Most people marry because they want to get married. For love, to have children—

for a whole host of reasons. And I manage to find the one guy on earth who's not after love. He's searching for a virgin bride because that's what his forebears did. You know what? It's downright archaic!"

"Stop." Zac held up a hand and straightened beside her. *Stop?* She hadn't even begun. She opened her mouth to protest his high-handedness. "I—"

"Stop right there," he cut across her. "Let's talk about why you think I don't love you."

"Oh, come on, Zac." She pushed up off the sofa and took a couple of steps away. "There's no need to pretend anymore."

"Isn't there?" he asked enigmatically, watching her through half-closed eyes, his legs stretched out in front of him.

"No." She threw him an assessing look from under her eyelashes. Straight talk? It was now or never. He'd have no choice but to let her go. She drew a deep breath. "Anyway, it would appear that you've been under a misconception."

His gaze sharpened to a bright, brilliant green. "A misconception?"

"I was not a virgin on our wedding night." Raising her chin a notch, she met his gaze and held her breath.

He went white. The shock reflected in his eyes made Pandora's stomach clench. Any hope she'd had that he'd dismiss her lack of virginity with a wave of his hand disappeared.

No, Zac would never have married her if he'd known she wasn't a virgin. That much was clear from the accusing glitter in his eyes.

He uncoiled and rose in a smooth, swift movement. The anger in his gaze devastated her. Suddenly Pandora felt tired and old and thoroughly disillusioned. "So now you see why there's no point talking…or keeping me on this island."

Zac's jaw moved, but no words emerged from between his lips. And his face reverted to hard and blank. In his silence she had her answer.

"I'm right, then." Her shoulders hunched and she drew a protective shield around the hurt inside her heart. "You don't love me—you never did. You simply *pretended* that you did. You lied to me, Zac."

"This is where I get to tell you that you're not the only one who feels cheated." His mouth twisted. "You haven't been wholly truthful, either."

"Where did I lie to you?" Pandora demanded.

"You had me believe you'd led a sheltered life—"

"I have! I spent half my life in St. Catherine's—"

He rode over her. "And now you reveal you are not a virgin."

"Oh, for goodness' sake." Pandora rolled her eyes to the ceiling. "How many virgins have you known, Zac?"

His gaze slid away from her, toward the darkening sky outside the vast sheets of glass. "That is not a question I'm prepared to answer." A dark flush lay along his cheekbones.

"I'll tell you how many—none."

His head came around. "How did—" He paused, then shrugged.

"It's obvious." Pandora threw her arms wide. "That's what this is all about, isn't it? That's why you're in this fix. Because there aren't any suitable virgins out there. Not unless you want to marry a fifteen-year-old and look like an utter pervert because you married a schoolgirl less than half your age. That's why you picked me. For some reason, you thought I was the perfect candidate."

The flush of colour drained from his skin and the pale flesh stretched tautly across his cheeks like alabaster. He stood unmoving, like the marble statue at the Acropolis Museum she'd thought he'd resembled, staring at her with those disturbingly empty eyes.

She held up an index finger and noticed absently that it trembled. "One lover. That's all I've had before last night. One lover."

And it had been a stupid mistake.

She'd been innocent, a silly little fool. But how could she explain that to Zac? He would never understand. She'd been so young and so darn gullible. Seventeen—nearly eighteen—and madly in love for the first time in her life. Pandora felt a stir of guilt. She hadn't given a thought to what her crazy infatuation might one day cost her.

It was going to cost her Zac. What was the point of skirting around the issue? That was what was at stake here. Zac had expected to marry a virgin. And she bitterly resented that he couldn't see past her lack of virginity to the woman who loved him with her whole flawed heart.

So when he took a step toward her, she backed to the door. In case her resolve melted and she dissolved into his arms, yearning for his love.

Her hands warding him off, she warned, "Stay away from me. You're not touching me tonight. I don't want to be in the same room as you."

And then she spun away from Zac and hurried out of the room.

* * *

The gurgle of the last of the single-malt scotch running into his glass led Zac to the realisation that he'd drunk the whole bottle he'd unsealed several hours earlier. Lurching to his feet, he stumbled to the deck, where he hurled the contents of the glass far into the night, revolted by his excess.

His wife was driving him to drink.

But tonight there was no need for Dutch courage. Pandora would not be waiting for him in his bedroom. Hell, he didn't want to remember the look on Pandora's face when she'd rounded on him, making it more than clear he wasn't to go near her tonight. So he'd arranged for Maria to prepare her a smaller bedroom down the other side of the corridor.

But not even his wife's biting anger could stop him growing hard and hungry at the memory of their wedding night. Last night his beautiful bride had wanted, revelled in the passion he'd shown her.

Yet now she hated him. While he craved her.

He sank down onto the couch and shook his head to clear it of the alcoholic fog that hung over him.

His wife. He'd been so desperate to get his hands on Pandora in the lead-up to the wedding day, but he'd waited. Restrained himself because he'd wanted it to be perfect for his bride.

The wedding had been perfect. And his wedding night had been even more perfect. He dropped his hands into his head. Pandora had been so responsive to his touch but so obviously lacking experience. So tight when he'd penetrated her. There'd been no reason to doubt that she was a virgin. Hell, he hadn't expected an intact hymen, not with the active, sporty lifestyle a modern girl led.

But he'd been floored by her announcement that he wasn't her first lover. The whole dream had blown up in his face, scattering pieces of chaos everywhere. Zac gave a groan. And he didn't know how to put his orderly world back together again. No wave of a magic wand would turn Pandora back into a virgin.

There had never been a divorce in his family in a thousand years. Not even his failure of a father had committed that sin. Zac rubbed a hand over his face, mentally recoiling at the idea of all that ugliness.

His head ached thinking about the choice. A sullied bride? Never! The scandal of a divorce? He could not let Pandora go.

If he flew her to the airport tomorrow, he'd never see her again. Never hold her, never touch her. He closed his eyes at the wave of nausea that swept him at that thought. Pandora was not going anywhere. Not until…

Until…what? He shook his head and another wave of nausea swirled around him. Hell, he couldn't think straight. Couldn't think what to do next. The sheer lack of clarity shocked him. With a wretched sigh, Zac reached for his glass—then remembered he'd tossed the contents over the edge of the deck and groaned. Collapsing sideways, he slid full length onto the couch and closed his eyes.

And wished that the room would stop spinning around him.

Five

The following day, a tentative knock roused Pandora from the doze she'd floated in for ages since dawn. Instantly awake, she swung her legs over the side of the bed, intensely aware of the slither of the pale gold satin nightgown against her legs.

Could it be Zac? Her pulse picked up. Could he be coming to apologise for not loving her, for misleading her, for all the grief he'd caused her?

"Who is it?"

Her query was overridden by another—louder—knock. Annoyed, she called, "Go away, Zac."

But the knocking continued to staccato against the door. Pandora leaped across the room, her heartbeat racing in anticipation of the battle to come. She turned the key in the lock and yanked the door open.

But it wasn't Zac who stood there. Instead, Pandora found herself facing an elderly woman balancing a breakfast tray on one hand, the other poised to knock again. Pandora recognised the bag and scarf slung over the woman's shoulder as her own.

This must be Maria, Georgios's wife. Pandora hid her exasperation and the twinge of disappointment that it wasn't Zac. "Oh, thank you. I must have left them downstairs last night."

Maria said nothing. Pandora tried not to let the woman's lack of welcome get to her. Instead, she scanned the teapot and cup, the bunch of dark purple grapes, the toast and conserve prettily arranged on the tray and said, "That looks delicious," before reaching for the tray.

Maria held on to it. For a moment Pandora thought the old woman intended to keep possession of it, then unexpectedly she relinquished it. Backing into the room clasping the tray, Pandora smiled her thanks.

Setting the tray on the chest of drawers beside the window, Pandora turned to find Maria in the room. The handbag had been set down on the bed. Pandora's silk scarf lay across Maria's hands, and the old woman's crooked fingers moved in little circles against the brightly hand-dyed silk.

Pandora warmed to her. "It's beautiful, isn't it? My favourite scarf."

Maria ignored her, her fingertips continuing to caress the fabric.

"Did Zac instruct you to give me the silent treatment? Is this another part of his kidnap plan? Isolate me? So that I fall into his arms?"

Nothing. Not even a glance from the other woman.

Pandora gave a sigh of impatience. "You know, a little politeness goes a long way."

At last Maria looked at her.

Pandora shook her head in disgust. "You're very rude," she said clearly. Shrugging when she didn't get a response, Pandora stalked to the door and pointedly opened it fully. There was no mistaking the message, and Maria's expression clouded over. She gave the scarf one last stroke before draping it on the post at the bottom of the bed. Then she shuffled past Pandora, her dark eyes veiled.

"Have a nice day." Pandora pinned on a wide smile.

But Maria didn't look at her again—nor did she deign to reply.

Shutting the door behind the rude old crone, Pandora locked it for good measure. Only then did she unzip her bag and realise that her cell phone was missing. She remembered Zac suggesting seductively that she spend her time on the island making love. She'd dropped the phone and he'd picked it up. The frustration simmering inside her notched up another degree.

Zac had kept her cell phone.

Seething, Pandora pushed open the curtains and blinked against the bright September sunlight. The absence of shadows made her glance at her watch. It was already midday, so she hastened to the en suite to wash and afterward pulled a floaty white sundress from the wardrobe where someone—Maria perhaps?—had hung her clothes.

Once dressed, she dragged an armchair from the corner of the room and placed it squarely in front of the window and settled down to tackle the fruit Maria had brought. She had just finished the grapes when a new volley of knocking thundered against the door. A moment later the doorknob rattled, but the lock held.

"Unlock the door." Zac's voice held a dangerous edge.

"Go away, Zac."

"Open it now," he demanded.

She stared mutinously at the door. A heavy thud rocked the door. But the wood held. His shoulder? Probably. She hoped it hurt like blazes. "Stop it, Zac."

"Open the damned door or I'll break it down."

At the thought of Zac's breaking the door down a forbidden flare of excitement stirred. *God, what was she becoming?* "If you use any force on that door, I'll lose the last tiny shred of respect I have for you."

There was silence. Then she heard him heave a heavy sigh. "You've hurt Maria's feelings."

The totally unexpected attack took her aback. "*I've* hurt Maria's feelings?" *What about her feelings?* Slowly she rose from the chair and went to unlock the door.

Her eyes widened as she took in Zac's appearance. He looked haggard. His normally tanned skin held an unhealthy yellow tinge, and his eyes were red-rimmed.

"Are you ill?" The words burst from her.

"Why?" he asked guardedly.

"You look terrible."

His gaze slid away from hers and he muttered something that sounded like, "I feel terrible."

"What?" she asked, frowning at him.

"It doesn't matter. What matters is that Maria is offended."

"I'm offended! That woman is rude."

"Don't talk so loudly." He flinched and half closed his eyes.

"You're hungover!" she accused.

He blinked but didn't deny it.

"You didn't see her. She was rude and insolent and ignored everything I said to her. She didn't even greet me."

"It's not her fault—"

"Of course it's her fault," Pandora cut in heatedly. She raised an eyebrow. "Unless you put her up to it?"

"I didn't put Maria up to anything. But I should've told—"

"You should tell her she needs to be more polite to me." Pandora cringed when she heard the self-righteous words and added lamely, "After all, I am your wife."

Zac stared at her as if he'd never seen her before. "Why do you deserve Maria's respect when you gave her none? She says that you opened the door, made her unwelcome in your room and slammed the door on her. That woman has been there all my life. She raised me when I lived with my grandfather at the house in Athens. She looked after me while my father went through dozens of floozies and my mother drank herself to death." Zac's eyes were flashing now. "One thing I never had you pegged for was a spoiled little rich girl."

"I'm not a spoiled little rich girl. She was damn rude to me. *She* ignored *me, she* turned *her* back on *me.*" It sounded so petty. It was obvious Zac cared about Maria. A lot. "Look, maybe she's worried now that you're married," Pandora conceded. "Maybe any woman you married would never be good enough in her eyes. But she didn't have to—"

"She's deaf."

"Deaf?" Pandora gaped at Zac. The scene in the bedroom ran through her head. "Oh, no! Now I feel terrible."

"It's my fault," Zac sighed. "I usually sign to her, although she can lip-read Greek fluently. I should have warned you to speak English very slowly and keep to a basic vocabulary. But I never even thought about it. I never think of her...disability."

"I'll tell her I'm sorry." Pandora lifted her chin. "But you're right—you should've told me. In fact, you should never have brought me here. What do you think Maria would think of the boy she raised abducting a woman?"

"You're not telling her that."

"I can't, can I? Not if she's deaf and can't lip-read English properly." She gave a mirthless laugh, furious with him, with her helplessness. "You've got it all sussed, right down to the deaf jailer."

"Kiranos is not a jail."

"It sure feels like one. Unless you're planning to take me to the airport?" Pandora sneaked him a look from under her bangs. But for the first time she wasn't so sure she wanted to go. Once she left, their marriage would be over. And Zac would never look at her with that glow in his eyes, never again touch her with fingers that reduced her to shivers—

God, she had to stop thinking about...about the sex side of their marriage.

Zac avoided her gaze. "I'll let you go when I'm good and ready."

His high-handedness caused another flare of annoyance. "And then you wonder why I say I hate you."

The eyes that met hers were a flat, expressionless green. "You don't hate me."

Before he could expose the ignominious desire she was trying to hide, Pandora retorted, "What's to like about you? You're arrogant, deceitful and sly. You talk about your noble ancestors and their chivalrous love for their brides, yet you abduct me and stop me from going home to my family. You are a man totally without honour."

Zac stared at her, his face ashen. Without a word, he swung on his heel and left her room, the door closing silently behind him.

Feeling no relief at her victory, only emptiness, Pandora slunk to the armchair and listened as his footsteps retreated. The tearing sense of loss splintered her soul, hurting deep within her psyche and leaving a void where her love for Zac had flourished. All that was left was the humiliating knowledge that she still wanted him. But after her last crack, he'd have to be made of steel to even think of touching her.

Dropping her head into her hands, she remembered Maria's sullen face when she'd left earlier…and just now Zac's face had been grey as a result of the words she'd hurled at him. Words that left the nasty, bitter taste of shame on her tongue. She'd always been kind and upbeat to everyone she'd met. At school, some of the girls had sniggered that she was a regular little Pollyanna. What the hell was happening to her? What was she becoming?

Yes, Zac's behaviour to her had been unacceptable. His actions had instilled a sense of confusion and powerlessness. And, yes, she'd been wallowed in her own misery. But there was no need to take it out on Maria.

Or even Zac. His shattered expression flashed through

her mind. She'd known that her words would hurt like poisoned arrows. Zac's sense of honour lay at the heart of the man he was—the man he believed himself to be. Her venomous attack had been small-minded, not like her at all. She'd behaved like a petulant child.

Remorse stabbed at her. And while a niggling voice said that he deserved it because he'd taken away her right of choice, her freedom, she suppressed it. She was not going to allow Zac's actions to destroy the person she'd always prided herself on being.

So when Maria arrived with her lunch tray, Pandora gave her a tentative smile and mouthed, "I'm sorry."

The Greek woman's face broke into a smile and she started to speak in very broken, very hesitant English. "Zac tell me you not know."

The knowledge that Zac had taken the blame for what had happened completely flummoxed her, and she stared after Maria openmouthed as she set the tray on the chest of drawers.

After Maria had gone, Pandora picked at the Greek salad with its red tomato quarters and fat olives before pushing the tray aside. Not hungry but not yet ready to venture out and face Zac, Pandora picked up a book. It was a mystery featuring a kick-ass heroine by a favourite author who usually held her entranced. But today the words on the pages aroused no interest.

The afternoon was hot. Even inside the thick whitewashed stone walls, Pandora could feel the temperature rising. The fine cotton dress clung to her body, so she turned up the air-conditioning. Thoroughly restless now, Pandora crossed to the window and pushed it open.

The villa—if one could call a structure with towers and parapets that—perched like an eyrie high above a sweeping cobbled terrace, and far below lay the stony beach. And beyond, the sea glittered in the sunlight. On the terrace, a thickset man with a head of unruly black hair—Georgios, Maria's husband, she supposed—was watering terra-cotta pots full of bright magenta geraniums.

The startling glare of the heat shimmered off the white walls of the villa. The sea looked blissfully tranquil. Incredibly tempting. Pandora stood there, her arms folded on the wide sill, for what seemed forever.

At last she acknowledged to herself that she was waiting for Zac to appear.

Turning away in disgust, she threw herself down on the bed and stared at the wooden door.

This time she hadn't locked it.

Because after her cruel words she knew Zac would not return.

Pandora spent the next three days closeted in her bedroom, avoiding Zac, full of remorse at the way she'd spoken to him the last time she'd seen him. But she couldn't help being a little irked that Zac hadn't bothered to check on her.

Yet beneath the conflicting emotions lay something more, an unsettling desire that was still very much alive. Despite everything he had done—and her own vehement demand for a divorce—what she really wanted was for Zac to apologise, preferably on his knees, for keeping her here against her will. It infuriated her to be so confused, at the mercy of a man and her own turbulent emotions.

The only respite from the quagmire of emotions, ironically enough, was Maria. Three times each day Maria brought her a tray heaped with delicious food. Swiss muesli and fruit and rich, creamy yogurt with honey for breakfast. Greek salads topped with chunks of crumbled feta cheese and glossy black kalamata olives, pita bread with *taramasalata* and hummus and slices of warm lamb seasoned with rosemary. Maria clucked like a concerned mother hen if she failed to finish meals and smiled her approval when the plate and bowl were clean of food. Any thought Pandora might've had to undertake a hunger strike to make Zac realise how seriously angry she was about what he had done was undermined even as it took root.

Maria brought Pandora a pile of outdated magazines. *Cosmopolitan, Harper's Bazaar* and *Town & Country,* as well as an assortment of Greek magazines, giving Pandora something to do. So one evening, when Maria arrived with a dinner tray, Pandora gave her the silk scarf she'd touched with such reverence that first morning.

Maria's eyes lit up. "Mine?"

Pandora nodded.

Maria took the scarf, holding it like some fragile piece of glass. Then she stood in front of the mirror and tied it around her neck.

"Here, like this." Pandora moved to Maria's side and fiddled with the ends until they were arranged to her satisfaction.

The smile of joy on Maria's face brought a lump to her throat. The old woman's wrinkled fingers kept going up to stroke the lustrous silk with reverent touches.

"Beau…beautiful." Maria struggled with the word.

Pandora dipped her head in acknowledgment. "It was

my mother's. She was an artist—she hand dyed the colours herself." She'd said too much—Maria's frown indicated she did not follow.

"Your mother…dead?" Maria asked finally.

"Ne." Yes. It was one of the Greek words she'd learned over the last few weeks.

Maria shook her head from side to side, muttering something in Greek, her hand going to where the knot sat at her shoulder.

"No." Stilling the older woman's hands, Pandora said, "It gives me pleasure to give it to you."

Maria seemed to get her meaning. *"Efgaristo."* And danced out the room on light feet.

Over the last three days Pandora had reread the meagre selection of books in her baggage, scanned the year-old magazines Maria had brought her until they were dog-eared, her heart stopping each time Zac stared unsmiling out of a photograph at her.

Now, as she readied herself for bed, Pandora finally admitted that she was bored out her skull.

So when she woke on Friday morning, Pandora stared out the window at the pebbled beach that edged the stony outcrop below the villa and decided she'd had enough of being cooped in her bedroom while the sun shone outside.

Quickly she donned a brief white-and-silver swimsuit and covered it with a white cheesecloth shirt that Zac had bought for her at the Plaka in Athens, then tied a yellow sarong around her waist and trod into a pair of metallic leather sandals. A slather of sunscreen, a hat, and she was ready to face the blistering Mediterranean sun.

She met no one as she crept down the spiral staircase and

bypassed the reception rooms. Outside, the beach was even more alluring than it had appeared from her window. The sea was a clear turquoise under the arch of cerulean sky. Round pebbles stretched into the water. Pandora found a flat rock and spread out her towel and stretched out in the morning sun.

What was Zac doing right now? Just thinking about him brought back the unresolved tension between them. She hadn't seen him since he'd left her room, white-faced, days ago. Where was he? She hadn't heard the helicopter depart, so she assumed he must still be on the island.

When was he going to release her?

Surely he'd need to return to the corporation he headed? Or did he maintain a makeshift office in the villa—despite his claim that Kiranos was his retreat from the frenzy that he existed in? From under the hat she risked a glance at the villa and scanned the windows overlooking the beach. Eventually she homed in on the three windows a level below the vast glassed living room. If an office existed, it made sense that there would be some sort of telephone, even a satellite phone—he couldn't be totally out of contact with the rest of the world.

With a sigh, she pushed the thought from her head and closed her eyes.

A little later, made lazy by the sun, she explored the beach, hopping along the pebbles to where a sheer wall of rock ended the curve of beach. Soothed by the gentle lap of the water against the pebbles, Pandora came back to where her towel waited and wedged herself in the shade of a large rock and closed her eyes.

That was where Maria found her when the sun was at its zenith. The tray of sliced fruit and fresh bread with slivers of smoked salmon and chunks of cheese looked delicious, and she thanked Maria. Made hungry by the salty air, Pandora ate with gusto. But she couldn't help wishing that Zac was here…to share the moment.

When she pushed her plate back onto the tray and pulled out the serviette wedged under a plate, a piece of folded paper fluttered onto the beach.

She bent down to pick it up.

Don't forget it is hot in the sun. Stay in the shade or come inside. Join me for a drink on the terrace this evening.

Pandora didn't need the slashed *Zac* to identify the writing.

At once a host of emotions shook her. Aggravation at his high-handedness. Regret for what might have been. And finally outrage.

How dared he leave her languishing for three days and now tell her what to do and demand her company? She ignored the twinge of fairness that admitted that staying in her room had been her choice. Deep down, she'd wanted him to come running after her, to placate her.

But he hadn't.

His failure to do so had both infuriated and frustrated her. Yet at the same time she was filled with a kind of relief. The past few days had given her much-needed breathing space and a chance to gain perspective.

She slopped on more sunscreen, telling herself it had nothing to do with Zac's directive about the heat of the sun, then lay down. But too soon she was hot and itchy. A sheen of perspiration dampened her skin. She wriggled and twisted. But the edgy feeling would not leave. Finally she rose and headed for the sparkling sea.

The water was cool against her heated body, the pebbles smooth under her toes as she edged carefully in. The water crept higher as she went deeper, and finally the unbearable frissons against her sun-warmed skin forced her to dive headlong into the calm water. She came up breathless from the mild shock of the saltwater. Swimming a little way, she turned onto her back and stared at the unfathomable blue of the sky overhead until the on-edge tightness subsided a little. She felt calmer, more able to deal with Zac.

Zac had been watching Pandora from his study on and off the whole morning—and it had shot his concentration to hell. Unsettled, he struggled to read the report his PA had e-mailed to him, a report that had to be finalized—he glanced at his watch—in the next half hour.

Pandora had called him a man without honour. And she was proving to be right. What did he care about a report deadline when Pandora floated on the sea in the tiniest wisps of white fabric bound with provocative silver bows that he itched to untie?

But her words rankled.

Because there was more than a hint of truth in them. Kidnapping her, bringing her to Kiranos when she'd clearly thought he was taking her somewhere to talk before allowing her to leave, had been devious.

He'd intended to talk her into staying married to him, to show her what they had going for them. And then she'd dropped her bombshell.

And it had all gone to hell.

Zac's gaze narrowed on the inert figure of his bride floating on the sea, only the occasional splash revealing she was awake. All his life he'd known he had a duty to fulfill. He was the Kyriakos heir. He would not fail the family as his father had. He would select a wife carefully when the time came. His bride's virginity was not negotiable.

Pandora had put her finger on the heart of his quandary: *That's why you're in this fix. Because there aren't any suitable virgins out there.*

He'd never been drawn to shy, simpering virgins. Since his twenty-first birthday, his family had paraded inexperienced sweet things in front of him—and none had stirred a response. It had taken Pandora, with her sharp wit and gentle beauty, to reach that part inside him that he'd always considered unassailable. He'd been so sure he'd found the answer to his prayers.

Except it had all been a cruel illusion.

He watched as Pandora rolled over in the sea and started to swim toward the shore.

Pandora was not pure in body. Telling himself that a sullied body didn't mean that her heart was any less pure did not help. He'd been misled. Although it was probable her father had believed his daughter to be untouched.

It was his own fault. He should have asked her outright before proposing. But he'd been too intent on getting her into his bed.

He'd been only too eager to accept she was a virgin.

So what if he'd known about her…flaw…from the outset, before he'd offered her marriage? Would it have changed anything? His head told him he would never have married her. Generations of Kyriakos men had married virgins. It was part of their identity, part of the rich heritage they stemmed from.

Part of the magic of the legend.

Yet his body was wired differently from his brain. Those few innocent kisses during their courtship had hooked him. Taking her to his bed and making love to her had been the most earth-shattering experience of his life.

How could he just let her walk away? Yet keeping her would rock the family to the roots and go against the tradition that his ancestors had established. A knot of pain formed under his heart.

Zac was surprised to discover that the thought of living without Pandora was more disturbing than her lack of maidenhead. Somewhere along the line, his priorities had shifted. He no longer really cared that he hadn't found the last virgin bride. He no longer cared about the Kyriakos legend. Not if it was about to cost him his wife.

He watched as she waded through the shallows, picking her way between the pebbles to where her towel lay. The sun glinted off her blond hair and turned her skin to a light bronze. Zac shoved his hands into his pockets.

What did his wife's lack of virginity matter? By marrying Pandora, he'd made her virginity a universal truth. The newspapers had speculated for years about whom he would eventually marry, running articles with accompanying photos of the young heiresses he might favour with a proposal and publicly knocking them off the list when they fell from grace.

He'd made damn sure that Pandora never saw the spate of stories that had followed his announcement of their marriage on her arrival in Athens. Stories headlining her purity to the public.

The tight knot in his chest started to subside. Her lack of maidenhead would be a secret he'd keep from his family—that way there would be no risk of the story leaking into the papers, making a mockery of who he was and destabilising the stock prices. No one else would ever know the truth.

Except…

He hesitated, watching as Pandora wrapped the towel around herself. Pandora had said she'd only ever had one lover. To date, the guy had not come forward—despite the enormous publicity of their marriage.

He'd find the man. Offer him enough money to silence him forever. He would do it for Pandora.

Yes, it was possible.

And he'd use this time on Kiranos to convince Pandora that they were perfect together. But first he had to overcome her fury and hatred. He just hoped he hadn't left it too late.

After the cooling swim, Pandora returned to her room and showered the last traces of saltwater from her body before slipping into a sleek white cotton sundress with a halter neckline. From her window she watched Georgios set two deck chairs out on the terrace. Zac appeared from the house, and her breathing quickened. He paused, said something to Georgios that made the old man laugh.

Pandora skittered back, not wanting Zac to see her. But he didn't glance up as he made for the steep stone stairs that led to the boathouse to the right of the beach.

Quickly she left her room and ran down the spiral stairway. She branched off on the level where she suspected Zac's study might be. Two doors opened off the small landing. Her heart in her throat, she opened the first and found a gym stocked with Nautilus equipment. The second door opened into a light, airy room that was clearly set up to be an office.

It was empty.

No sign of Maria cleaning…and she'd seen Zac heading for the boathouse.

Her gaze hurriedly scanned the desk, the bookshelves, taking in the bank of computer ware, the clean, organised surfaces…but no sign of her cell phone or Zac's.

About to leave, she noticed the flicker of the screen saver. Feeling like a thief, she scuttled around the desk and perched on the edge of Zac's big black leather chair. With a sense of nervous elation, she hit the enter button and waited.

A document opened. Zac had not logged out. Fingers shaking, she minimised the document and hit the Internet connection icon. A home page opened. Relief and a kind of shaky guilt made her sag. She cocked her head. Only silence. No sound of the pantherlike tread of Zac's returning footsteps.

She tapped in a Web-mail address and waited a moment before keying in her log-in and password.

Pandora stared at the screen. A list of unread messages sat in her in-box, several containing subject headers congratulating her on her marriage. No time to read them now.

Hurriedly, she clicked on the new message tab and typed in her father's e-mail address. After a moment's reflection, she filled *Need your help* into the subject line. It was much more difficult to find the words than she had expected. She wanted to tell her father that her marriage was over, that she needed him to rescue her from this mess.

But how to explain it all? She hesitated. How could she tell her father that she'd lost her virginity after some stupid visit to a nightclub with a man she'd barely known three years ago? Her father had trusted her to go stay with Nicoletta and to behave as he expected. How could she disappoint him?

And what would happen about the lucrative contract her father had signed with Zac? He'd walk away from it, putting her first.

No, she couldn't let her private failures screw up her father's business relationships. She had to sort this out herself. Her twenty-first birthday was less than a month away. She was an adult now, not a child who needed to run home to Daddy every time something went wrong.

Zac had brought her here against her will. To talk, he'd said. She'd been bitter, too angry to talk, and had flung her loss of virginity in his face. The diversion had worked. And she'd retreated to her room to sulk, wasting three days waiting for him to come seek her out.

It was way past time to grow up, to take control of her life and her future. She had to find Zac and have it out with him.

But first she owed her father a chatty, upbeat e-mail. He'd been so happy about her marriage. With a small sigh, she started to type.

"What the hell are you doing?"

Pandora jumped when Zac's voice exploded behind her. Spinning the high-backed leather chair around, she blurted out, "E-mailing my father. He'll be worried—and hurt—if I don't keep in touch."

"Daddy to the rescue," Zac said, but the deep lines of tension around his mouth receded.

"I don't need my father to fight my battles."

The glint in his eyes changed to something that she thought might be reluctant admiration. Then he spoiled it by saying, "I want to read what you have written."

Her chin went up. "Don't you trust me?"

His eyes flickered to the screen.

Pandora scooted the chair forward, blocking his view of the screen. "It's private, my communication to my father. I'm simply assuring him that I am well and that we are on an island—how do you spell Kiranos by the way? It would look strange if I didn't get it right."

After a fleeting hesitation Zac, spelled it out.

"Thanks." Pandora bent her head and continued to type. Tense now, she waited for Zac to move closer, to peer over her shoulder…to stop her sending the e-mail. But he didn't move. Finally she clicked the send button and looked up. "Done."

Zac was watching her, a bemused expression on his face. "I'm reputed to be a suspicious, hardheaded bastard. I can't believe that I trusted you to do that." He shook his head and held out a hand. "Come, let's go sit on the terrace and see the day out."

As Pandora rose and took his hand, a deep inner tension unwound and a delicious warmth spread through her. But she suppressed the treacherous want that unfurled inside her.

She and Zac needed to talk.

Six

"Zac, if you can trust me to e-mail my father, then surely there's no point in keeping me prisoner on this island?"

The sun was still hot on the terrace, but the shadows were starting to lengthen. For a moment Pandora thought Zac wasn't going to respond and that the words she'd flung at his broad back would be lost in the sea wind.

Then Zac swung around from where he'd been leaning against the white railing at the end of the cobbled terrace that overlooked the Ionian Sea and let the binoculars fall. "Kiranos is hardly a prison. You didn't enjoy your swim earlier today?"

Pandora slumped back in the deck chair Georgios had set out on the terrace along with a couple of side tables. If she were honest, she had to admit it was a pretty luxurious prison—her every whim catered for. Behind Zac, the sea lay blue and inviting. But it was a prison nonetheless. She lifted a shoulder and let it fall. "Swimming wouldn't have been my first choice of things to do."

"So what would have been your first choice of… things…to do?" The suggestiveness in his richly sensual tone made her flush.

"Certainly not *that*."

His gaze raked her, reminding her of the skimpiness of the fitted dress, with its shoestring halter neckline that left her shoulders bare and dipped to reveal a generous amount of curving breast. In the wake of his gaze, the heat ran riot.

He flashed her a grin. "Sure about that?"

"Yes," she bit out, resenting the effect he had on her body. She couldn't help noticing how cool and assured he looked in a pair of cargo shorts and a white Polo shirt. "I'm sure. There's lots better stuff I could be doing at High Ridge right now."

"You'd walk away from a stay on a Greek island, sunning yourself on a private beach, in favour of winter in New Zealand? Where it's bone-cold right now?"

Pandora hunted his face for signs of sarcasm but found none. "What good is a Greek island when you're only there as a hostage?" she said at last.

"You're not a hostage." Zac looked annoyed. The grin had disappeared. "Tell me, have I hurt you? Tortured you? Locked you in your room? Starved you?" With every word he came closer.

"No." She stared back at him, challenging him. "But keeping me here against my will—it's barbaric."

Zac shrugged. "So I'm a barbarian. Greek legends are full of tales of abduction. You need look no further than Orpheus—"

"Who took Persephone to hell!"

Zac gestured to the calm stretch of blue sea and the silver sunlight streaming down on to the water. "This is hell?"

"No. Yes. Whatever. It's not where I want to be. What you're doing is against the law. I'm going to report you to Interpol the first chance I get." He looked remarkably unconcerned about her threat, even though she knew it was an empty one. He hadn't hurt her, and she didn't really want him incarcerated for kidnapping.

"So where do you want to be, *agapi mou?*"

"Stop it! Don't call me *My love* in that phony way."

His jaw clenched. "I'm not going to argue with you in this mood." He lifted the strap from behind his head and held out the binoculars. "Here, take a look, there's a school of dolphins out there."

Anger forgotten, Pandora reached for the binoculars and came to her feet. "Where?"

"Under the swarm of seabirds."

"Oh, I see them. Five…seven…no, eight. I see about eight. There must be more underneath."

"It's a big school." Zac spoke from behind her, and she tried to ignore the fact that he stood so close that the scent of his skin enveloped her. "They've been frequenting the island for years. I recognise the big bull with the chip out his dorsal fin."

"This is wonderful. We get them at home. Whales, too. But it's lovely to see the dolphins here, as well. And such a big school. Oh—" she squealed. "Did you see? One just jumped out of the water."

"It's great to have them out there. That's why I pour

millions into coastal and ocean conservation each year. So that their survival is assured."

With the binoculars against her eyes, Pandora said, "But you own supertankers and transport crude oil. Isn't that a contradiction? What if there is an oil spill?"

"The Exxon *Valdez* incident was a tragedy. But it increased everyone's awareness of the danger to the environment. My supertankers are among the safest in the world. While all tankers are vulnerable to storms and human error and mechanical failure, mine are part of the new breed that are double-hulled for greater stability."

In the sea, two dolphins arched over the water. Zac watched her squeal with delight, his mouth curving into a smile—her pleasure was infectious.

"It gives me such a kick to know they're there." She lowered the binoculars and looked at him, the laughter fading from her eyes. "You know why that is, don't you?"

Zac didn't think he wanted to know what had caused the happiness to fade from her face, but he could see from the battle gleam in her eyes that she was intent on telling him. "Why?"

"Because they are free." She handed the binoculars back to him. "You need to let me go, Zac."

Zac looked away, unable to hold her defiant gaze. He didn't answer. If he let her go, would he ever see her again? Or would this consuming force between them be lost to him forever? How could he explain the corrosive fear that if she left, he'd be alone for the rest of his life?

He couldn't utter those words. Because she was all wrong for the man he'd been raised to be. So he swung around and strode away.

Five minutes later, his face annoyingly clear of expression, Zac returned from the villa carrying a tall frosted glass filled with amber liquid that looked like beer in one hand and a small sherry glass in his other hand.

Pandora eyed the tiny glass of sherry Zac held out to her and a surge of rebellion rose within her. A sudden urge of devilry prompted her to say, "That looks like something my great-aunt Ethel would drink on a cold winter's evening in front of the fireplace at High Ridge. I'd like a margarita, please, with crushed ice and lots of salt around the rim. And don't go too light on the tequila."

Zac did not look pleased. "Sherry is what the women in my family traditionally drink before dinner."

"Not this woman. Perhaps you should ask what I like to drink?" She cast him a quick look. His jaw was tight, his lips pressed in a thin line. "In fact, cancel the order for a margarita. Make it a Sex on the Beach. Please."

For a moment Zac looked stunned, then his eyes turned molten.

Pandora backtracked furiously. "It's a cocktail…made with vodka, peach schnapps, orange—"

"This is not funny," he interrupted. "My wife does not order such things to drink."

"It wasn't meant to be funny." From behind her fringe she tried to gauge his mood. "And I won't be your wife for much longer." Zac scowled and he loomed over her. She stuck her chin out, defensive now. Her attempt to put him in his place had backfired on her. Badly.

She tried to make amends. "Look, I can't drink wine. It gives me a headache. Spirits suit me better."

Some of the dark turbulence left his eyes. "Would a gin and tonic do?"

She nodded. "Even just tonic water with ice and some lime would be good." And she heaved a sigh of relief as he headed back to the house. She let her body sag in the deck chair and tried not to think about the sudden flare-up between them. Her resentment and ongoing urge to needle him weren't helping matters.

Zac returned with a long glass. She took a sip—it was cool and tasted of fresh lemons with the tiniest hint of juniper berries. "Thank you."

"Pandora…" Zac gave his head a shake and sank into the deck chair beside her, stretching his long, tanned legs out in front of him. "We've gotten off on the wrong foot. Believe me, I want this marriage to work." His eyes were intent, greener than she'd ever seen them and desperately serious. "I want it to be a real marriage, with you at my side."

"How can this be a real marriage if you won't let me go? If you stand over me when I e-mail my father? If you won't even give me my damn cell phone back?" She gave a sigh of exasperation when he didn't answer. "And all because of some random family legend, right?"

"It's not that random," he said, and she could feel the waves of tension coming off him from where she sat. "But you know what? Somehow the legend is not important anymore."

"Not important?" She set the glass down. "When you believed that I'd be the perfect patsy to marry?"

His brows drew together. "It wasn't like that."

"It was *exactly* like that. You convinced me that you

loved me. You married me because you thought I was a virgin. Who told you that, anyway?"

"Your father."

"My father?" She gaped at him in shock. "I don't believe you."

"I don't lie." The distaste in his tone quelled her instant response. "Your father wanted this marriage to happen. I was in Queenstown for an ecology conference. We met. He told me all about you—he's very proud of you. It was no secret that I needed a wife—the right wife."

"A virgin bride, you mean?"

He gave a slight nod.

How humiliating! The whole world knew Zac needed a virgin bride. No wonder he hadn't wanted her reading the newspapers after their engagement was announced. The tabloids' speculation must've been lewd. And her father had put her up as a pure-as-driven-snow candidate. Ack. Suddenly Pandora was fiercely glad she'd decided against e-mailing her father for help. Of course, her father didn't know about…the incident.

"So everyone knew about this…virgin deal…except me. I was stuck in the backcountry bush, looking after guests at High Ridge, while you guys plotted my fate. God, it sounds so feudal." She hauled in a deep breath and covered her eyes with her hands. "And I thought it was fate. True love. Jeez, you must have thought me a silly, gullible little fool."

"I thought you were exquisite. Sweet, charming, funny. I wanted to share my—"

"Stupid. That's what I was," she interrupted him, dropping

her hands and fixing him with a determined gaze. "A world-class idiot. So how are we going to fix this…this disaster?"

His eyes flashed. "It need not be a disaster. We can work it out. But first I want to hear about this man."

"What man?" But she had a horrible feeling she knew exactly what he was talking about.

Zac's deck chair scraped across the terra-cotta cobbles. He leaned toward her and held her gaze squarely. "The one who claimed your virginity."

"Zac!" Pandora gazed at him in fascinated horror. "You can't expect me to talk about that."

"Oh, yes, I can." His brows drew together, and the dusky evening light that fell across his face dusted his harsh features with gold. "You might not have lied to me intentionally, but you've put me in a situation I never anticipated. I need to know the full facts to put a game plan in place to cope with any possible fallout."

She stared blindly at the pink-and-orange clouds scattered across the western sky. This wasn't about her, about her dignity, about her future with him. This was about *him*. About *his* business. About a fortune in share losses. About how *he* was going to handle their divorce…except he'd said he wanted to stay married, hadn't he? She shook her head to clear it of the confusion and the ugliness.

Her relief when Georgios appeared to tell them dinner was ready was short-lived. No sooner had they made their way to the dining room and sat down at the table, where the silver cutlery glinted in the glow of half a dozen tall white candles, when Zac demanded, "Talk to me."

"Okay," she said in a flat little voice, and picked up her fork to toy with the seafood salad in front of her. "I'll tell you exactly what happened. His name was Steve. He was charming, fun, good-looking—"

"I don't want to hear that part," Zac growled, a muscle pulsing high on his lean, tanned jaw. "I want to know who his family is, where you met this man."

"I don't know anything about his family," Pandora said awkwardly, uncomfortable with the turn the conversation had taken.

"So how the hell did you meet him?"

She stopped picking at her food. "Sometimes my father allowed me to spend the August vacation with my best friend, Nicoletta. Her father was a very wealthy industrialist. They came from Milan, and a couple of times I stayed at their holiday home in Sardinia. A few times Nicoletta stayed with us. But High Ridge in winter isn't as much fun as Sardinia in summer, so that didn't happen often. She had an older brother—"

"Ah," said Zac.

Pandora glared at him. "Alberto was only interested in soccer. There was no time in his life for anything else."

"Then tell me about this man who—"

"I'm getting there."

"Too slowly."

"Zac! This is very difficult for me. Let me tell it my way, okay?"

Zac inclined his head. "I'll be quiet."

Pandora could see him visibly forcing himself to relax. It did nothing to calm her. She pushed her plate away and drew a steadying breath. "Nicoletta's parents told Alberto to escort us around, to be a good host. Nicoletta loved frequenting the fashionable beaches to work on her tan and flirt with Alberto's friends. I was horribly shy. But I went along with it because I wanted to fit in. Alberto tolerated the beach. In his view, it was better than taking us shopping. So each day Alberto would take us to play volleyball with a group of his friends—friends his parents approved of as fit company for Nicoletta—on the beach at Costa Smeralda. I started to come out my shell. It was fun."

"I'm sure it was," Zac growled.

"Zac, you said you'd be quiet!"

"I find it is impossible. What were your friend's parents thinking allowing you and their daughter to be exposed to all these young men?"

"They came from wealthy families, some had minders. Even Alberto and Nicoletta had a bodyguard. He was young—Alberto wouldn't tolerate an older guard—and just as mad about soccer and sports as Alberto. That's why Alberto put up with him."

"Don't tell me the bodyguard—"

"No, no, nothing like that! Give me a chance to finish, Zac." Pandora couldn't hold back her impatience any longer. "That's where I met Steve. On the beach, playing volleyball with Nicoletta, her brother and his friends. Alberto didn't know Steve, but they discovered they had an acquaintance in common."

"I bet they did."

"Zac! Anyway, Steve was good at volleyball. But he was different from the other guys—he talked to me and Nicoletta. He was interested in what we had to say."

Zac pushed his plate away. "I'm no longer hungry."

"Me, neither," Pandora muttered.

Zac let out his breath. The sound was loud in the silence

of the darkening room. "It couldn't have been hard to pick out a bunch of rich young kids. He must've had his eye on a rich wife."

"I didn't see it that way. He seemed so sophisticated. But, remember, I was not yet eighteen and he was twenty-five. He wore clothes with a cachet none of the guys I knew did. He drove a sporty red Alfa. He was very European, very cosmopolitan."

"I don't want to hear about your adolescent fantasy." Zac sounded fit to burst, and the muscle was back in play, working high on his jaw. "I want to hear what happened."

Pandora closed her eyes to avoid looking at him.

This was so much harder than she'd expected, reliving her stupidity, telling it all to Zac. "You have to understand…it happened precisely *because* he was an adolescent fantasy. I'd never dated. Goodness, I'd never been allowed to go anywhere with a boy. I didn't even get to meet any. I had no brothers. I was at a very strict girls' school. My father was very protective. Steve looked nothing like the kind of guy I'd been warned about. He was good-looking, obviously smart and successful and he wasn't a threat. I could lust after him to my little beating heart's content."

There was silence.

Pandora opened one eye, then the other, and slid Zac a sideways glance. He was glaring ferociously, his jaw working like mad. She took a deep breath and plunged on. "He was more interested in Nicoletta. She'd always been more sophisticated, more developed physically, too. But he was nice to me, polite."

"I'm sure he was." Zac snorted.

"He was! He was interested in what movies I liked, the books I'd read and in hearing about the kind of girl stuff guys usually ignore. He even knew how compatible our horoscopes were. We used to joke about it—especially because he fancied Nicoletta. And he took me and Nicoletta shopping. He knew all the best shops. He would give advice while we chose shoes and bags at Prada and clothes at Versace. He was fun." And she'd been enchanted.

"Sounds like a gigolo." Zac glared at her, the candle flame throwing his carved cheekbones into sharp relief.

"Zac, he wasn't. I certainly never gave him money." But she had bought him a pair of sunglasses he'd admired. And a wallet. Nicoletta had bought him a leather jacket—in spite of his protests—and some other frivolous items that had caught her eye. Pandora had signed some of the tabs when they'd gone to lunch, the three of them—she, Steve and Nicoletta—while Nicoletta had picked up others. They'd thought it empowering. Steve had joked how he liked twenty-first-century women.

"He talked us all into going clubbing." Pandora remembered her excitement, how it had felt to be seventeen and falling in love for the first time. This time it wasn't a crush based on a poster of a movie star or a photo of a school friend's brother. This time it was the real thing. Except she'd thought nothing would come of it because he'd so obviously preferred Nicoletta.

She'd been so naive.

"So he took you to a club and got you drunk." Zac made a growling sound. "Two young girls."

"We didn't go alone." She glared at him. "Let me finish. Alberto and the bodyguard came with. The first time we went, we only stayed for about an hour and we danced most of the time. But the next time we went, another friend of Alberto's arrived, a guy Nicoletta had always fancied. Steve was heartbroken."

"I'm sure he was," Zac muttered. "He must have been crying in his Jack Daniel's at the thought of the fortune slipping through his fingers."

"You're such a cynic. He wasn't like that!"

"Did he know how wealthy you were?"

"I don't think so. I was on the edge of the circle, the quiet, shy one."

But she hadn't been so shy that night that Nicoletta had gone off with Luigi. Then, she'd been animated—courtesy of the sweet, colourful cocktails with outrageous names she'd drunk to loosen her inhibitions. The excitement had carried her forward recklessly. When the seduction had come, she'd fallen into Steve's bed like a ripe plum.

"Afterward…" Even the memory of her enthusiasm was mortifying. Jeez, she'd even invited Steve to High Ridge. "I wanted him to meet my father. I started talking about how soon we could get married. I mean, that's what I thought love was about. I was so sheltered it was frightening. He couldn't get away fast enough. I went back to New Zealand with my tail between my legs."

"Idiot!" But Zac looked thoughtful now. "And that was the only time you slept together?"

She nodded miserably.

"Did he ever contact you again?" The intensity in Zac's voice told her this was important. She snuck him a look across the table. His face was tense, unsmiling.

She thought of the messages her father had passed on

to her when Steve had tracked her down and called her home in New Zealand a month later stating he needed to talk to her, that it had all been a misunderstanding.

Thank heavens her father had no idea what had really happened. She'd told him only that Steve was a friend of Nicoletta's brother, Alberto. That's when her father had told her that he'd had a trace done on Steve's number, had him checked out and had decided he was an unsuitable companion for his only child. That he wanted her to cut the connection. Pandora had agreed with alacrity—Steve had made it painfully clear that last time she'd seen him that he didn't feel anything like love for her. That her silly crush was not reciprocated. The last thing she'd wanted was her father to discover exactly how stupid she'd been, how she'd let him—and herself—down.

"No," she said, stretching the truth a little, justifying it to herself. After all, Steve had never actually spoken to her.

"And you never heard from him again?"

She fiddled with the corner of the linen napkin. "What's the point of all this? It's not going to change the fact that I'm not a virgin." Pandora wanted the inquisition to end. It achieved nothing except to stir up humiliating memories of the silly little goose she'd been.

"Humour me. Did you ever see him again?"

She shot Zac a quick glance. His face was set, his gaze persistent. He was not going to let it go. And she no longer wanted to talk about it.

"He's dead," she said very quickly, throwing the napkin down and crossing her fingers under the crumpled fabric.

Zac tensed, his body vibrating. "Are you sure about that?"

Pandora glanced away from his piercing gaze into the

blinding flicker of the candle flame. "I told you," she said tonelessly. "He had contact with Alberto through a friend. That's how I heard."

"I assumed his claim to know a friend was a con on the part of this Steve to gain access to Alberto's circle of friends."

She'd never thought of that at the time. How naive she'd been. No wonder her father worried about her.

"Okay," Zac said slowly. "So does anyone else know what happened that night?"

"I never told Nicoletta or Alberto…I was too ashamed." And racked with guilt because she'd coveted a man who fancied Nicoletta. "And I doubt Steve would've, either."

"No, he'd have wanted to keep open the chance to cement a relationship with your friend, Nicoletta, the wealthy industrialist's daughter," Zac remarked a trifle drily.

"Can we let it go now?" Pandora pleaded. "It was a mistake. I was so young, so romantic and so utterly stupid."

"The memory is painful—"

"*Yes.* I wish it had never happened. I moved on afterward—it was my mistake, my secret. I went to the doctor. That in itself was terrifying because I had to find a doctor that my father didn't know." It had involved deception and made her feel underhanded and defiled. "I confessed to the doctor that I'd had a one-night stand and that I was scared I might be pregnant. I was so naive I didn't even know if Steve had used protection that night."

She'd been distraught. The doctor had been sympathetic. She'd done a pregnancy test and sent away samples for tests for diseases that Pandora had never even heard of.

"I told myself that I'd been lucky. I'd made one mistake,

but I hadn't gotten pregnant, nor had I picked up any disease or infection. So I put the whole nasty experience behind me. I refused to let it wreck my life." Pandora blinked back the tears that filmed her eyes. "Yet now that night has come back to haunt me."

"Pandora," Zac's tone was urgent.

She met his gaze staunchly. Zac would not want her now. She would get her divorce and go home to High Ridge. *But at what cost?*

"That one night means I'm not fit to be your wife."

"Pandora!" Zac's hands reached across the table and closed over hers. The shadows from the candlelight played over his face, giving him a dark, mysterious edge. "There is a way. The only people who know about your… indiscretion…are you, me and the doctor who is bound to silence. The man involved is dead."

Something, some dangerous emotion, fluttered under Pandora's breastbone. "What are you saying?"

"I'm saying that we keep it a secret. The doctor's not going to tell nor will I. No one need know that you're not a virgin."

"Would you do that?" Did this sacrifice mean that Zac loved her? He was going against his entire upbringing— everything he'd believed in—to keep her with him. "Would you stay married to me? Keep the truth from everyone? Even your sister?"

Zac looked torn. "What choice do I have? It's too late to annul our marriage—it's already been consummated. If I walk away from you, the paparazzi will tear you apart. How can I do that to you? We have no option but to make this marriage work."

Her heart plummeted at his response. How wrong she'd been. He didn't love her at all. But his sense of honour wouldn't allow him to throw her to the news hounds.

How could she live with him for the rest of her life knowing her marriage was a sham?

"I don't know…" She hesitated.

If she left and returned to High Ridge, she'd never see him again. Never see that slow, sexy smile light up his eyes. Never experience the heart-twisting kisses again. Did she *really* want to walk away from him forever?

No.

"What have we got to lose?" Zac ran his thumb along the base of her palm, and tingles ran up her spine. "We have a certain chemistry between us already."

She blushed. "Marriage is about more than sex, Zac. It's about common goals and values." *And most of all, it was about love.* She'd always dreamed of marrying a man who loved her above all else.

"Sex is a damn good starting point." His slow, sizzling smile made her heart turn over and her pulse rush into overdrive.

How could she resist him in this mood? Did it matter that he didn't love her? Zac wasn't a fortune hunter. And, despite what she'd said, he wasn't cruel or barbaric. He loved his family. He was a good man, a man of principle, the kind of man she'd dreamed of marrying.

Could this simmering sexual connection between them be enough, as Zac had suggested? Should she take a chance and hope that he'd learn to love her?

"We'll take it slowly, one day at a time," Zac was saying. "And if you stay, let's get to know each other a little more. I don't expect you to share my bed right away." But his gaze had dimmed a little as he'd added the final words.

"You'd do that?"

"This is important to me. Give it two weeks here on Kiranos. At the end of that time, we talk again. Nothing is lost. If you still want to go, you can walk away and go back to your life in New Zealand. I'm offering you your freedom."

"You'd let me go?" Her heart sank. For some ridiculous reason, that wasn't what she'd wanted to hear; she wanted him to fight for her, convince her.

"I won't keep you against your will. I brought you here to talk, to ask if you would consider staying for a while so that we could get to know each other a little better. Unfortunately—"

"Unfortunately I told you I wasn't a virgin."

"That confession made things a little…difficult," Zac admitted, his eyes hooded from her gaze. "I needed time to come to terms with your revelations."

When his gaze met hers again, she thought she glimpsed something in the depths of his eyes, something vulnerable, uncertain. Then she dismissed it. Zac uncertain? Never!

"And what," she asked, "if after two weeks I decide I want to…to leave?"

"We go our separate ways for a year or so and then file for a quiet, low-profile divorce. I'll do my best to protect you from the media backlash that will follow. Being in New Zealand will help—it's a world away."

It sounded so simple. She could do that. Spend two weeks on Kiranos relaxing, enjoying Zac's company.

"You'll have no pressure of any kind. No lovemaking. Just the sun and the sea and spending some time getting to know each other all over again." Zac echoed her thoughts. "To see if it can work."

Except he omitted the one thing that she found herself thinking about most. His impact on her…

His touch.

His kisses.

And, above all, his lovemaking.

Disappointment curled inside Pandora. Their wedding night had been so exciting, a storm of passion. Nothing had prepared her for the wonder. The experience with Steve had not come close. Then, she'd been tipsy, filled with guilty excitement, and it had been over before it had started, leaving her feeling more than a little cheated. With Zac it had been different…

But Zac was right. A lot had passed between them. This was a chance to start over. To see what they had. All she had to do was sit it out on an island paradise and then she could walk away—if she chose to—without involving her father.

It wasn't even as if she was at any risk. Zac had made it clear he expected nothing from her—not even sex. Nothing except to give their marriage a chance.

"Okay," she said. "Now can I have my cell phone back?"

"Okay? Just like that?" He gave her a long look. "And why do you want your cell phone?"

She shrugged. "There's no reception, so it won't be much use to me. But think of it as a gesture of good faith."

"Agreed." A strange smile played around his mouth. He reached into his shorts pocket and drew out her small, shiny silver cell phone and held it out to her. "And now you can give me something."

Pandora hesitated, the glint in his eyes warning her. Then she took the phone. "What do you want?"

"A kiss." His smile widened. "Think of it as a gesture of good faith."

Seven

"A kiss?"

Zac didn't answer. But the teasing glint in his eyes challenged Pandora. He expected her to refuse. He was laughing at her, darn him.

Recklessly, she blew out the nearest candles, leaving only one fat white candle burning on the sideboard, then she rose and leaned over the table toward him. "All right."

Placing her hands on his shoulders, Pandora pressed her lips against his…and waited. He stayed motionless. Yet her own response flared wild and primal in her belly, and her breath came more quickly. The velvety darkness surrounding them intensified the sensual mood of the candlelight. Beneath her palms, his Polo shirt had become a barrier that prevented her from caressing his sleek skin.

She moved her hands in urgent little circles against the fabric.

Under her mouth, his lips moved. A sigh. His? Or hers? She didn't know…and didn't care.

His body heat rose through his shirt, warming her hands, and his scent was intoxicating.

Pandora's breathing became ragged. Parting her lips, her tongue stroked across the seal of his lips in a bold caress.

Zac's body tensed, coiling into a tight, expectant mass of bone and muscle and man.

She repeated the soft stroke.

He groaned and his mouth gave under hers. The only sound in the room was their ragged breathing. Her fingers tightened on his shoulders.

At last Zac pulled away. "You are so beautiful." The hand that stroked her hair away from her face shook. "You are kind to Maria—yes, she told me you gave her a silk scarf you valued. You think of your father worrying about you. Your heart is pure."

She thought of the lie she'd told him and her hands slipped from his shoulders. She forced a smile. "You're embarrassing me. I'm far from perfect. And I did consider asking my father for help. But I decided against it." And she squirmed inside.

"Pandora." Holding her a little distance away from him, he said, "Zeus, this is hard for me, but I'm not going to break my promise to give you time. I'm not going to make love to you."

His eyes were clear of everything except an intensity that drew her in, making her aware that he was male and she was his mate…and nothing else mattered.

"I'm not going to rush you into something that might be a mistake. I want you to be very, very sure. Understand one thing—I want this marriage to work, okay?"

Slowly she nodded.

The next week passed in a daze of sun and sea and sleep. As part of their two-week truce, they'd fallen into meeting before breakfast for a run along the footpath that wound past the pebbled beach in front of the villa and then curved away from the beach, between the olive trees up to the headland, before descending to a sandy cove on the other side. The sand in the secret cove was soft and silky, so different from the pebbled beach. Zac would strip off his singlet and charge into the water, and Pandora would drop her towel and follow at a more sedate pace.

Since kissing him at dinner, Pandora found it increasingly difficult to ignore the effect Zac's briefly clad body had on her. She seemed to have developed an inner sensitivity to his closeness. Each morning when they swam out and around the tall rock that jutted out from the sea, she was intensely aware of the smooth, easy stroke of his arms cutting through the water beside her.

Once back in the shallows, she struggled not to gawk at Zac as the droplets streamed off him, his broad muscled chest sheened by moisture and his skin golden in the sunlight. She was tempted to kiss that full, smiling and deliciously sensual mouth, but she didn't dare in case she unleashed a force that she could not control.

Instead, she would run up the beach, pull on her sneakers and grab her towel before tearing down the pathway. Zac would laugh, then she would hear the thud of his footsteps behind her. Eventually she would slow her pace to a jog through the olive grove, absorbing the clatter of the cicadas as the heat started to rise.

Back at the villa, she would veer off to her room for a cool shower, so that by the time she joined Zac for breakfast she was composed enough to face him with no sign of her craving hunger for him. After breakfast, Zac would disappear into his study, leaving Pandora to amuse herself for the rest of the day by listening to music, reading or sunbathing at the beach or watching DVDs from the huge collection Zac owned, while inside her the glow of desire smouldered unslaked.

By Friday Pandora had exhausted Zac's library of DVDs. It was after watching *Zorba* that afternoon that Pandora said rashly after dinner, while they were drinking strong Greek coffee in the glassed room, "Teach me to dance."

Zac got the reference instantly. "You've been watching *Zorba*."

"Yes, and that's not all. Although, I gave the soap operas a miss. Maria said she watches them."

"That's where she's learned the little English she knows. She loves them." Zac's eyes smiled as he spoke about the old woman. "So what else have you watched?"

"*Strictly Ballroom, Take the Lead* and *Shall We Dance?* You have an interesting selection."

"Katy loves dance movies." His gaze turned watchful. "Are you bored?"

"I'm not used to doing nothing," she said honestly.

"We'll remedy that. When we get back to Athens I'll introduce you to Pano, the CEO of Kyriakos Cruises, and perhaps you can develop an active role in the South Pacific region of our tourist-cruise program."

Pandora shot him a sideways look. He made it sound as if her agreement at the end of the two weeks was a foregone conclusion. Did Zac know how tempted she was to stay married to him? Even though he didn't love her?

But she wasn't ready to surrender quite yet. So she tracked the conversation back to dancing. "Remember at our wedding…you said you'd teach me to dance some of the more complicated dances?"

Zac pushed the coffee table back and moved to the bank of stereo equipment, and a few seconds later the sound of music filled the air.

"Come," he said.

Pandora rose. For a moment fear rode her and she wondered if she'd gone too far too fast. Then she stepped forward to where Zac waited and lifted her arms.

"The *hassipikos* is not like a lot of other Greek dances. We start slowly. Once the music speeds up do we change over to a faster, spiralling dance. Now, stand beside me. Here."

Pandora obeyed.

"Get ready to take a step forward. Left foot this time— not right, like most other Greek dances." The music changed. "Now."

Confidently, she stepped forward.

"Good," said Zac. "Two more steps, then we're going to move sideways. Watch my feet."

Pandora was laughing by the time they got through the next section of music, the sweeping arm movements, the complicated crossover steps.

"Let's try that again." Zac flipped the track back to the beginning. "Ready? Now wait for it, then the steps."

Pandora stood still, her arms stretched out and linked with his. She thought about what Zac had said during their wedding about listening to the music, about letting it take her. She heard the tempo change and started forward, the gliding, swaying steps with Zac beside her.

The music swelled, the singer's voice rose. Then she and Zac were moving sideways, their bodies perfectly in time, in tune, yet not touching. A sense of wild exhilaration filled her at the accomplishment.

"I did it! I can do it." She threw her arms around Zac. "Thank you." Her lips smacked his cheek. "I want to do it again."

Zac had gone utterly still.

Pandora pulled back. Too late. Emotion raged in Zac's eyes. Self-consciously she dropped her hands from his shoulders. Zac's hands shot out, circled her wrists and yanked her close.

"You're not going anywhere."

And then his head sank. His lips slanted across hers, hard and hungry. No longer gentle and exploratory, as on their wedding night. No longer immobile and waiting, as when she'd kissed him after dinner a week ago. Now his hips moved against her, his erection unhidden. This was the full masculine hunger unleashed. And it aroused her. Unbearably.

She gave a hot little moan into his mouth. The music was picking up, the rhythm quick, building to a climax.

It brought back the memories of their wedding night. Of the dancing. Of what had followed…his hands on her skin, her body writhing under his.

"No!" Zac tore his mouth from hers. "I gave you my word. Only another week still remains of the two weeks I promised you. Then I will demand my answer."

"You're refusing to make love to me unless I give you the answer you want?" She glared at him in mock outrage, her body objecting as he held her away.

A hard grin slashed his face. "Yes, I have to use every advantage at my disposal to get what I want. *You*."

The days passed swiftly, and by the following Tuesday Pandora was the rich, golden colour of honey. A sensual glow filled her as she smiled across at Zac. They'd just completed their run to the sandy cove she'd begun to think of as their secret place.

Four days left. On Saturday morning Zac would demand his answer. And Pandora knew what she was going to tell him.

She watched him covertly as he shrugged off his singlet and waded out into the sea. When the water lapped the edges of his shorts, he dived forward and came up ten yards farther ahead. He flicked his wet hair away from his face and called out to her, "Aren't you coming in?"

What was the point of waiting? She knew what she wanted. She wanted Zac, inside her, here, now. Pandora's heart knocked against her ribs at what she was contemplating.

Before she could chicken out, she stripped off her T-shirt. Then slowly, with hands that shook, she tugged the bows that fastened her bikini bra loose. She let the skimpy top fall to the ground. Reaching up, she pulled out the hair tie that held her hair in a sleek ponytail. Bundling the mass together, she secured it with the stretchy tie on the top of her head, her breasts lifting pertly, the nipples tight from the excitement that pulsed inside her.

Finally she shot Zac a glance where he stood motionless in the sea. Pandora's nerve almost gave out. In the bright sunlight, his face was hard, the bones standing out in sharp relief under the taut tanned skin. She looked away and headed for the water, forcing herself not to hurry, aware of the undulating sway of her hips and the movement of her unrestrained breasts.

The sun was warm on her bare breasts, and the cool water rippled against her knees…rising higher as she walked steadily deeper…pooling between her legs… cooling her belly. With relief Pandora sank into the silky water and started to breaststroke into the deeper water, still refusing to look in Zac's direction.

But she could sense his stillness. Sense the tension winding tighter in him. So she stroked a little faster, her gaze fixed, unwavering, on the tall rock in the sea ahead. She heard the splash behind her and broke into freestyle. A quick glance over her shoulder showed her the flurry of Zac's arms powering through the sea, gaining on her, and she started to swim in earnest until her heartbeat resounded in her ears.

She didn't make it to the rock. It was still ten yards ahead of her when Zac's hand closed around her ankle. He yanked. She went under and surfaced a moment later, sputtering, as he forced her to the surface.

"What are you—" She didn't finish. His mouth covered hers, wet and cool and salty.

She gasped, her feet floundering, searching for the sea bottom, out of her depth in more ways than one.

Her legs brushed against his thighs, and desire bolted through her as she felt the hardness of his arousal.

He lifted his head and she gulped in air. "What are you doing?"

Pandora smiled into his eyes. By stripping off her brief swimsuit top and brazenly swimming past him she'd broken the pact between them and raised the stakes.

The days of inane chitchat had worn her down, and the egdy awareness under the banal social chatter had been rising, twisting higher and higher. She was tired of waiting.

"I want you." She moved against him.

He groaned. "Don't do that. We have an agreement."

"I know what I want. I want you. I want to stay married to you."

He stilled. "Are you sure you don't want to be free?"

"I want to be your wife."

Then his mouth took hers again, his hands framing her face. Tangling her legs with his, Pandora let her body go heavy and was rewarded as they sank, the water closing over their heads.

Zac worked his arms to take them to the surface, but Pandora countered by wrapping her arms around his upper arms. She opened her mouth. Her tongue slid into his mouth, her lips sealing against his to stop the water rushing in.

Zac had stopped beating his arms. The hair tie had worked loose and her hair spread around their faces as they spiralled lazily down, weightless in the current. Bubbles streamed past, diffusing through the blue-green world that encapsulated them.

The pressure started to build against Pandora's eardrums. She needed a breath, but she didn't want to leave the silent blue world where Zac floated warm and solid against her.

This must be what it felt like to be a mermaid, Pandora thought hazily and licked at the cavern of Zac's mouth. Then his legs kicked and they jetted upward. They broke the surface and broke apart, gasping for air.

"Are you trying to drown me?" He slicked his wet hair off his face.

For the first time since she'd met him she felt as if she had the upper hand. "I've never been kissed under water." A breathless exhilaration filled her and a reckless rush of adrenaline pumped through her. She grinned at him.

"Well, I'm glad there's something where I could be first."

Instantly the lighthearted euphoria evaporated. Was her youthful stupidity always going to come between them? Pandora turned away and struck out for the rock. She made it safely and pulled herself out, wishing desperately that she wore her swimsuit top. She folded her arms across her exposed chest.

When Zac reached the rock, he said, "I shouldn't have said that."

"No, you shouldn't." She pursed her lips and stared over his head at the white sandy beach.

"You look like a mermaid. A very beautiful, very sexy and, right now, mad-as-hell-at-me mermaid." The hand that he rested on her thigh made her jump. She struggled to ignore him.

"Look at me."

"Why?"

"I want you to see what you do to me."

"I felt…in the water." Pandora felt herself flush.

"I'm not talking about what you do to me physically. I want you to look into my eyes and tell me what you see."

She gazed into his upturned face. The reflected rays of the sun turned his eyes to jade, and a rivulet of water ran from his wet hair down the hard bones of his cheek.

"So what do you see?"

She shook her head.

"Tell me."

"I can't read you—you're too good at hiding what you feel."

"Then I'll show you," he said with a husky growl and dropped his head.

The sleek stroke of his tongue on the soft skin above her knee caused her to shriek, "Zac! Don't."

"Mmm, you taste of salt and sun and bright white heat."

Pandora shuddered but didn't object as his mouth touched her again.

Taking silence as assent, he moved higher.

She tensed…waiting. Her legs parted at his touch. He tugged at the little bows at her hips, and she sighed as the wet fabric gave and fell away. When his tongue touched her…there…she shut her eyes and her head fell back. She moaned, a hoarse, primal sound. She forgot about the hard rock under her bottom, forgot that she was naked, that he could see every intimate part of her, and her whole existence became focused on the sharp pulses of pleasure.

When the shudders came she gasped and tensed, then spun into a place that was hot and cold and the colour of silver. She opened her eyes, and his face, blazing with triumph, filled her vision.

"I could get addicted to watching you come."

She coloured, suddenly self-conscious, and shifted, closing herself to his gaze.

"Don't. You're beautiful. Like the heart of a flower."

"Zac, you're embarrassing me."

He rose up and with gentle care he lifted her off the rock, slid her slowly down his body until her thighs reached the water. She squealed at the cold and wrapped her legs around his thighs and buried her face in the arch where his neck joined his shoulder.

"What about you?" she whispered.

"What about me?" There was a hint of laughter in his voice, and Pandora was unbearably conscious of his hands cupping her bare bottom and holding her securely against him.

"Don't you want...to...to..." Her voice trailed away.

"Come?"

"Yes," she whispered, burying her face deeper against his skin and smelling the salt and residue of aftershave and pure male.

"We have the whole afternoon to make love."

That made her lift her head. "Here? On the beach?"

"Why not? We're all alone."

He bent and brushed a kiss over her mouth. Instantly her lips parted and his tongue sank into her. The kiss was deep. Intimate. Anticipation ratcheted up a notch and Pandora waited, her senses on fire. The hands on her buttocks tightened. She gasped and desire clawed its way up her spine. She wriggled against him, the hard stomach muscles rubbing the naked heat of her. He hoisted her a little higher so that the smoothness of his erection slid between them, sliding through the highly sensitive folds.

Shivers caught her.

The reckless desire soared.

"Now."

He laughed. "Be patient. We have all afternoon. We'll go back to the beach. I'll lay you down on it, then I'll kiss you here—" a touch that made her gasp "—and then you can have me."

Her head thrashed from side to side. "I don't want to wait. I want it now."

Zac's breathing grew ragged.

"Like this?" The blunt hardness probed her.

Pandora arched her back, sweat breaking out along her spine. "Yes," she hissed out. "Just like that."

He slid all the way in, and goose bumps of pleasure broke out over her skin at the intense sensation that swept her. She moaned and clutched at his shoulders.

He moved inside her. Pandora gasped. His hands relaxed a little, creating a space between them, and she felt him slide out, then he was pulling her close again, impaling her, the friction unbearable. Her pulse was hammering in her head, growing louder and louder until it became a roar.

Zac swore, harsh and succinct, and sank into the water, submersing them both below the surface. The sudden cold broke the daze of desire, and with a jerk Pandora realised the roar in her ears was real—not her heartbeat but the sound of a chopper. She yanked her arms from around his neck and crossed them over her breasts—way too late.

"Don't worry, they can't see us. We're in the lee of the rock." He held her locked against him, and the speed of his thrusts increased.

Pandora was torn between worry that they might be discovered—that the helicopter might sweep overhead—and the feverish escalating sensations that threatened to send her spinning into a climax.

"I can't hold back." His voice was hoarse. His hands tightened on her rear, pulling her closer still.

"Don't you dare—"

He was moving wildly against her, within her. "I can't hold anymore." And then he was shuddering, his large body trembling against her.

Pandora was aware of a terrible burning frustration before the sound of the beating rotors drowned out everything except the fear of discovery.

Zac swore. "Who the hell can that be?"

Pandora hoped frantically that Zac's assurance that no one except his family knew about his island hideaway was true. And that the paparazzi hadn't found them.

In silence they rapidly pulled on their clothes and jogged back to the villa. A helicopter bearing the logo of a commercial operator was partially visible on the helipad atop the flat roof by the time Pandora followed Zac up the stone stairs to the terrace and through the side door into the house.

She was excruciatingly conscious of her tousled hair and the wet patches where her T-shirt and shorts clung to her sea-dampened body, sure that anyone could see at once what they had been doing.

As the sound of a woman's voice reached them, Zac's pace increased. "What are you doing here, Katy?"

"Don't be so rude, brother dear." Katy shook her head. "Pandora, it's fabulous to see you again." Pandora was enfolded in a quick hug and an airy kiss landed on her cheek. Zac's sister stepped back. "Look at you, so tanned. You look wonderful." She drew a breath, bubbling with radiance. "I've picked up a little weight, can you see? The doctor said I was too thin—we're trying for a baby again."

Zac gave a sigh. "I suppose that means you won't come to your senses and leave Stavros?"

"Zac!" His sister pinched his arm. "Don't joke."

Pandora glanced from one to the other, trying to follow the byplay. She didn't think Zac was joking. He looked dead serious, his full mouth set in a hard line. What had Katy's husband done to deserve his ire?

"Where is Stavros? I don't suppose you left him behind in Monaco? Or at one of Angelo's resorts?"

"Zac! Don't be naughty. You know we've been in London."

Naughty? Pandora sputtered over Katy's choice of adjective. Zac was too male, too dangerous to ever be described as anything as boyish as *naughty.*

Katy was babbling on. "He's here. He's coming now. He wanted a quick shower. Be nice to him, Zac. For my sake. Please." Katy gazed up at her brother with soft, imploring green eyes. "He's trying really hard. He's promised me there won't be any more…slips at the casino tables."

"I'll believe that when I see it," Zac muttered sotto voce. Pandora glanced at Katy to assess her reaction to Zac's taunt. Either she hadn't heard the last comment or she'd chosen to ignore it. Deciding it was time to give Zac and his sister a little private family time, Pandora moved to the door.

"Where are you going?" Zac demanded.

"I thought Katy might appreciate something cold to drink in this heat."

"That would be lovely. Thank you, Pandora." Katy threw her a white smile.

"Maria will be up in a moment. Come sit down." But Pandora barely heard Zac. Her attention was riveted on the man walking through the door arch.

"Steve!" The strangled whisper died in her throat. No, it couldn't be. Not now. But the man looked horribly similar. Same curly black hair and brown eyes, same corded, lean body.

There was no doubt in her mind—it *was* Steve.

Older, a little softer, but still good-looking in an ivory-skinned, raven-haired, continental kind of way—and still very aware of the impact of his looks. He hadn't seen her yet; he was too busy directing that practised charming grin at Zac.

Of course, Zac didn't appear charmed at all. But then, Zac wasn't an impressionable almost-eighteen-year-old.

God, she'd landed in a nightmare.

She bent her head forward, hoping to remain unnoticed, peeping with fatalistic trepidation through her damp hair, her heart twisting in her chest, making her feel quite ill.

Zac had ironed the distaste out of his face. "Stavros, you missed my wedding. Let me introduce my wife, Pandora."

Finally Steve—Stavros, whatever his name was—looked at her. Pandora wanted to drop through the floor.

How could she have fallen so hard for this man? Next to Zac he looked so lightweight.

"Pandora?" Zac frowned at her.

"Oh, hi," she greeted breathlessly to make up for her lack of manners. *Please don't say anything,* she prayed.

Stavros was staring at her and she read the knowledge in his eyes. He remembered her. Damn. A quick brooding glance in Zac's direction, then his attention came back to her, a hint of malevolence in his smile. "It's been a long time. How are you, Pandora?"

The words were a death knell.

There was a horrid silence.

Then Katy said, "You know Pandora? What a coincidence. How nice for Pandora—she knows hardly anyone yet. Where did you guys meet?"

Pandora prayed harder.

Steve—Stavros, she amended—must have seen something of the desperation in her eyes, because he gave a dismissive laugh. "It was a very long time ago."

"It couldn't have been that long ago," Zac drawled. "My wife is not yet twenty-one and she was a schoolgirl not so long ago. Fill us in, Politsis. Please."

"Zac—" Pandora tugged at his sleeve. "Can I speak to you alone?"

"Now?"

"Yes." Pandora felt light-headed with shock. She must be white as a sheet.

A bride pure in mind. A bride pure of body.

God, why had she lied? She'd failed Zac on both counts. He would never forgive her, but she could try to explain....

Maria chose that moment to arrive with a tray of cold

drinks. Katy signed her thanks and took one off the tray with a big smile at the old woman.

Pandora edged to the door, dragging Zac with her.

Katy's glass clinked against the table as she set it down. "So where did you and Pandora meet? I can't remember you ever going to New Zealand?" Katy was asking her husband with interest.

Pandora quickened her pace, nerves balling her stomach into a tight knot.

"We met in Sardinia. Pandora was there with a group of friends."

Beside her, Zac halted, his biceps tense as steel under her fingertips.

"Zac, I need to talk to you," Pandora pleaded, desperation drumming inside her head.

"Wait."

Panic clamoured inside Pandora, cold and frightening. She tugged his arm again. "Zac, please…come."

"Oh?" Katy invited, sounding intrigued. "Did you know any of the girls? Anyone I know?"

"I'd become friendly with one of their brothers—we'd struck up an acquaintance on the beach playing volleyball."

Zac swung around. He shot Stavros a lethal narrow-eyed look and then the full weight of his attention descended on Pandora.

The green eyes were not warmly intent but slits of ice. She squirmed under his glacial gaze, then looked away, unable to handle the accusation there. She knew that she was flushed now, no longer pale. But the shocky feeling was growing worse. Anxiety and guilt must be written all over her.

"Pandora, look at me."

She shook her head.

"Look at me!" His voice was a whip crack.

She flinched. Her head shot up. There was distaste and rage and pain in his eyes. She swallowed and forced herself to maintain eye contact. *Zac knew.*

"You told me he was dead," he murmured through bloodless lips.

Eight

Pandora ran.

Locking herself into the guest bathroom, she bent over the basin, her temples throbbing. Not even the icy water she splashed on her face helped clear her head. At last the pulsing started to ease, and she straightened and stared at her wan reflection in the mirror.

She couldn't stay here all day. So after wiping her hands on a fleecy white towel, she moved to the door, pressed her ear against the dark-stained wood and listened.

Everything was silent. No shouting. But then, Zac was too civilised to ever do anything as uncouth as shout. Her heart hammering, Pandora opened the door a crack.

The sight of the man leaning against the wall made her start.

"Wait."

She relaxed a little when the figure morphed into Steve, not Zac. Warily she made her way out into the passage.

"You made a beautiful bride. The duckling has grown into a swan."

She was horribly conscious of her damp shorts, the clinging T-shirt and her hair hanging in rats' tails. "I didn't know Zac was your brother-in-law, Steve." *If I'd known, I'd never have married him.* But that didn't help an iota. Not now.

"It's Stavros, actually. Steve is the anglicised form of my name."

She ignored the explanation. "You weren't at the wedding. Did you know it was me?"

"How could I miss the photos plastered over every paper, in every magazine? Imagine my surprise at reading about my brother-in-law's luck at finding you—the rich, beautiful virgin who fulfilled the criteria of the Kyriakos legend."

Don't search for those photos in the newspapers tomorrow. The lies and half-truths that accompany them will upset you. Concentrate on us, on our future together. Zac's words came back to haunt her. And she'd thought them so romantic at the time, thought he was taking care of her... that he loved her. No wonder Zac hadn't wanted her reading the tabloids, hadn't wanted her to find out why he was marrying her. Another bit of her dream splintered.

"So you knew it was me." She eyed Stavros thoughtfully. He'd had the advantage of knowing they would meet eventually.

If only she'd had an inkling.

Fighting for composure, Pandora tried to get a handle on the queasy feeling in the pit of her stomach and cast around for a way to handle this gracefully. Right now she needed to get her mind together before the inevitable confrontation with Zac. "Look, I was very young then. It was over a long time ago."

"You wound me." His hand rested on his heart. "I tried to get in touch with you but your father—"

"Wouldn't let you contact me. I know. He told me. He thought you were an opportunist." She gave Steve a hard-eyed stare. Steve's mouth looked fleshy, self-indulgent, nothing like Zac's beautifully molded mouth. Had her father been correct? Had Steve been after her trust fund and her father's fortune?

Had Steve married Katy for her money?

"You mean nothing to me now, Stavros. You've got a wife, I've got a husband…" Her voice trailed away at the scornful look in Stavros's eyes.

"What?" she whispered. "Why are you looking at me like that?" The blood started to hammer in her head and she rubbed her temples.

"You won't have a husband for much longer. Zac's not going to want you now. You're soiled goods—and he's the Kyriakos heir. Your marriage is over, Pandora."

"What is going on here?" Zac came around the corner like a predatory cat hungry for prey, his eyes flashing accusingly as he took in how close Stavros stood to her. Pandora inched hastily away. "Is this a tender reunion of love rediscovered?"

The ache in her head intensified at the contempt in his voice. *Soiled goods.* She felt sick. "Excuse me."

"You're not going anywhere, wife of mine."

But Pandora had had enough. She plunged past Zac's outstretched arm and fled back into the bathroom and turned the key.

Pandora barely made it to the toilet before she started to retch, shock and horror causing her churning stomach to convulse.

When she opened the door again, Zac was waiting, his arms folded across his chest, his gaze hooded. Her heart sank like a stone. Of Stavros there was no sign.

Putting her head down, she brushed past him. Zac's hand caught her arm. "Pandora—"

"Not now, Zac." She wrenched away and broke into a run. By the time Pandora reached her bedroom, her heart was racing. But no footfalls followed.

Locking the door, Pandora ran a bath and added bath gel. But not even the frothy bubbles could lift her mood as, filled with self-recriminations, she sank back into the scented water.

What had made her lie to Zac?

Yes, that awful experience three years ago had been utterly humiliating. She'd wanted it erased from her life. Forever. And, yes, she'd sensed how important it was to Zac that Steve—Stavros, she had to get used to calling him that—was out of the picture.

Dead was as out of the picture as it got. It had seemed such a petty little white lie telling Zac that Stavros was dead.

As far as she was concerned, the damned man *was* dead. She'd never expected to see him again. So she'd lied on the spur of the moment. To make it all go away.

Not terribly clever. And now Zac would never forgive her. She'd lied to him, broken his trust. She had to come to terms with that. This time she'd gone beyond the pale.

The biggest irony was that more than anything in the world she wanted to stay married to Zac.

Oh, she'd been outraged that he'd brought her to Kiranos without her consent, angry that she'd been forced into a situation where she could not escape…where she'd been forced to listen to him. But none of that had stopped what she felt for him.

She loved him.

Pandora covered her face. *She loved him.* The past week and a half had been wonderful, the honeymoon of a lifetime.

Yet for Zac their marriage was one of convenience. Except, inconveniently, she wasn't the virgin he required. But against all odds he'd been adamant that he wanted her to stay, to give their marriage a chance, giving her a rock of hope to cling to that he might grow to love her. After all, he'd said he loved her sense of humour, loved her appearance, her intellect. That had to count for something.

Even though she'd failed him at every turn. *And how she'd failed him.* Pandora ran shaking fingers through her hair. He'd wanted a virgin. She'd slept with his brother-in-law. He'd wanted a wife he could trust. She'd lied to him.

Her loss of virginity was something she couldn't change, her maidenhood was gone forever. She didn't hanker after that. Her virginity—or lack thereof—didn't make her a worse or better person. *But she'd lied to Zac.* She'd told him that Stavros was dead. And that was something she could never forgive herself for.

She doubted he would, either.

It was hours before Pandora could bring herself to face Zac and the others again. Finally she went down to dinner, only to find that the meal was still half an hour from ready and that Katy and Stavros were already gone.

"I sent them away." Zac stood with his back to the wall of windows, a dark shadow against the waning light.

Pandora sank down onto the ivory leather and resisted the urge to burst into tears. "Your sister wanted to see you. Don't let this come between the two of you—I know how close you are."

"How can it not?" Zac didn't meet her eyes. His skin pulled taut across his slanted cheekbones. "Every time she comes to visit I will be forced to stare into the face of the man who took my wife's virginity."

"I'm sorry." It was a cry of despair.

He didn't respond.

"Do you want a divorce?"

Zac stared at his wife, shocked at the bald question. She was pale, her pink mouth the only hint of colour in a too-white face. The lower lip shook slightly, giving him some idea of how tough this was for her, but her remarkable silver eyes were steady as they held his.

She wasn't hiding from her lie. And she'd already realised the implications of it. He wanted to deny it, drum his fists against the wall, tell her that it didn't matter, because she was his wife, goddammit. That she'd always be his wife.

But it did matter. He was the eldest—the only—Kyriakos son. And he'd always known what his destiny had to be. Torn, he held her gaze, unable to utter the word that he knew had to be said. *Yes.*

But she must have read something in his eyes, because her teeth bit into her lip until he could see a white mark forming. He wanted to demand that she stop.

He moved. Instantly she drew her legs up until her feet perched on the edge of the seat and her knees formed a shield in front of her. "So Stavros was right. He told me that you'd want a divorce."

He wished he could get his brother-in-law's scrawny neck between his hands. Shake him. For the pain he'd caused Pandora.

He squared his shoulders. "I don't want a divorce."

"You don't have a choice. That's what Stavros said."

He hated that she'd been listening to Stavros. Hated that Stavros was right. Except he didn't want a divorce. He raked his fingers through his hair.

But how could he stay married to Pandora now, given the scandalous circumstances? If anyone ever found out…

Yet he'd wanted to stay married despite learning she wasn't the virgin he'd needed to marry, a little voice at the back of his head taunted. He'd been prepared to hide the truth of her lack of virginity then so that he could keep her. But that was before he'd discovered her relationship with Stavros. He sighed. "I need to think about this. I'm not going to make a hasty decision."

Her eyes widened. "You're not going to divorce me straightaway?"

"I'm not going to be rushed into a decision. I need time to absorb the fact that you had—" he paused "—intimate relations with my brother-in-law, to absorb that you lied about his death." He needed time to decide whether he could stay with a woman his brother-in-law had deflowered. Time to consider whether he could ever let her go. Time to calm down before he made the most important decision of his life. He dragged a ragged breath. "What else did Stavros say?"

"That—" She broke off.

The pain in her eyes damn near killed him. *"What?"*

"That I'm soiled goods."

"Damn him. I'm going to kill him."

"Zac! He's your sister's husband."

She was right. Yet the thought of Pandora with Stavros was driving him mad. He'd never felt like this about a woman. Possessive. Protective. "I can't believe you let Stavros—" He shook his head. "What is it about Stavros Politsis? My sister's so besotted with the bastard that I have no chance of convincing her to kick him out."

"You've tried?" she asked.

He nodded. "When they got engaged I tried to pay him off. He wouldn't take it. No doubt he rubbed his hands in anticipation of more to come down the road. He's not worthy of associating with our family." He pinned Pandora with his fiercest glare. "I want you to stay away from him from now on. I don't want you near him."

Pandora's shoulders stiffened and her eyes blazed. "Why would I want to go near him? He means nothing to me."

"Make sure it stays that way." Zac threw back his head and closed his eyes. "Tomorrow we return to London. Stavros's arrival has soured our stay here. I no longer have any taste to honeymoon."

The following afternoon Zac found himself glaring at Pandora where she'd curled up in the seat of the helicopter. The first he'd seen of her today had been after he'd sent Maria to summon her to the helipad.

Was she sulking? He couldn't forget the way her silver eyes had blazed at him yesterday after he'd commanded her to stay away from his sister's husband.

Zac slid into the seat beside her. "What the hell's the matter with you?" he said finally. "Why are you huddled up in a ball?"

"I don't like flying in these death traps."

"We'll be in Athens soon enough."

She raised her head and gave him a guarded look. "And what happens then?"

For a moment Zac said nothing. "I told you I need time. Don't force me to make a decision in haste about something as important as our marriage."

Her eyes widened in her ashen face. She looked even worse than she'd looked when she'd stepped onto the roof. Zac took in the trepidation in her eyes and for the first time started to wonder if she was afraid of heights—or flying. He pushed the notion away. No, it was unlikely. She'd flown all the way from New Zealand without a qualm. She was simply still angry with him.

He took his cell phone out of his pocket and pretended to be engrossed with the small screen.

But when she turned her head away and her shoulders started to shake, Zac felt something inside him give.

Pandora was crying.

"Pandora…" Her shoulders stiffened. "I know finding yourself face-to-face with Stavros could not have been easy for you—"

She swung around, her cheeks stained with tears. She swallowed visibly. "This—" she jabbed a finger at her eyes "—has nothing to do with Stavros, about what's happening between us. I hate flying, okay? It terrifies me."

Guilt spread through him. He remembered her hesitation on the roof, the bleak look she'd shot him before she'd clambered in. More guilt stabbed him as he thought back to her rage when he'd dumped her into the helicopter the day after their wedding. "You should've told me." He moved closer and brushed her silky hair off her face. She pulled away and he let his hand drop. "If you'd spoken up, I would've gotten you some medication to take the edge off the phobia."

"Drugged me, you mean? To make the kidnapping when you brought me to Kiranos easier?"

He felt his face grow tight at the barb. "You're deliberately misunderstanding me. I'm talking about now, not when I brought you here. A mild sedative would've made this flight easier."

"I don't need drugs. I shouldn't have had to make either flight—you should never have put me into a helicopter coming here, then I would never have had to endure it a second time." She felt so much better for chiding him. It helped take her mind off the fact that however long Zac took to think it through, there was only one outcome for their marriage: divorce.

"You need to get over this irrational fear."

She rounded on him. "My fear is *not* irrational. My mother died when one of these crashed."

He went still. "Dear God, when?"

"When I was seven." Zac had been sent away by his mother when he was six. Pandora resisted the burgeoning notion that he might understand a little of the loss and bewilderment her seven-year-old self had experienced.

"I didn't know," Zac murmured. "Neither you nor your father ever mention her."

"That's supposed to make me feel better? That you didn't dump me into a helicopter deliberately?"

"You should've told me."

"*When?* Do I need to remind you that I thought I was going to the airport to catch a plane? I can survive a trip in a jet."

"I'm glad to hear it. Because when we reach Athens we're going to transfer over to the Gulfstream to fly to London."

Pandora ignored him. "The first I knew of your intention was when I heard the damn thing hovering above me. I was slung over your shoulder at that point. Given the noise and my terror, I wasn't in the right frame of mind to give lengthy explanations. I begged you, damn you, to let me down."

"I thought that was because you didn't want to come with me."

"And that makes it better? You ignored my objections because you knew I didn't want to be kidnapped. Right?"

"Sarcasm doesn't become you."

She huffed out, "What do you expect? Submission? You've got the wrong woman. You know, I really should have you arrested. Think of what a juicy story that would make. I can already see the headlines. 'Desperate Tycoon Kidnaps Reluctant Bride.'"

He gave her a hard look. "You're joking, I hope."

She'd never have him arrested. *Never.* She loved him. She turned away from him—and found herself facing the window and the yawning emptiness tilting beyond.

"Help." Covering her face, she fought the surge of panic.

"Come here." He pulled her into his arms. "I'm holding you and I will not let anything happen to you." The scent of his body filled her senses and slowly the panic subsided only to be replaced by something infinitely more dangerous—the lazy curl of desire.

As they hurried through Heathrow, Zac kept an eye on Pandora, his brows jerking together. No wonder she hated him. Her mother had died in a helicopter crash, and straight after the strain of their wedding he'd thrust her headlong into the capsule of her nightmares. He'd win the Bastard of the Year award hands down. He told himself he couldn't have known, that he'd make it up to her.

But would she let him?

A sideways glance revealed that with her black coat pulled around her and her long pale hair streaming down her back, she looked washed out. Her face was grey, her silver eyes dazed.

When a photographer slithered toward her, Zac barged the guy out of the way and slung a protective arm around his wife's shoulders, shepherding her to the chauffeur-driven Daimler waiting outside.

Once inside, she turned her face to the window, presenting him with the back of her head. Zac hated this unspeaking silence. He could sense her misery across the space separating them.

This was not the provocative mermaid he'd pleasured in the sea yesterday. Briefly he wished they could go back to that moment, when they were the only people in the deserted cove. Before reality had arrived in the form of his sister and Stavros and the scandalous revelation that had changed everything.

* * *

Zac's London town house was located close to Hyde Park, in the heart of the city. As they passed through electronic gates set in a solid fence of cast-iron pilings and huge white pillars, Pandora caught sight of window boxes planted with lavender, which softened the stark white lines of the architecture.

The phone was ringing when Zac and Pandora walked through the huge, imposing wooden door into the town house. A moment later Aki appeared, said something to Zac in Greek, his gaze sliding sideways to Pandora.

Zac strode away. Pandora followed more hesitantly across the glossy marble floor. She could hear him talking on the phone, his voice guarded, his replies terse, ending with an abrupt, "No comment."

Pandora tensed. *Why were the press calling?*

She forced one foot in front of the other and entered what was clearly the sitting room. A warm-hued kilim lay on the floor between a pair of rich brown chesterfield couches and what looked like a Magritte hung over the fireplace.

Zac was standing with his back to her in front of a wide television screen, the handset cradled in his hands revealing that the call had been terminated, and his shoulders were hunched. His reaction offered little comfort and the tension knotting her chest wound tighter.

"Zac?"

He turned and looked across to her, his eyes so dark, so full of turmoil that her heart missed a beat. "Zac, what is it?"

"They know."

"Know what?" But Pandora didn't need his answer— she read it in the starkness of his gaze, in the sallow shade of his skin. She sank down onto the nearest couch and dropped her head into her hands.

"The press know about Stavros…that he was your lover before you married me." Above her bowed head, the citation of facts continued relentlessly. "They know that you were not a virgin bride. The paparazzi are questioning whether I knew, too—and misled everyone—or whether I, the Kyriakos heir, was duped." And then she heard Zac tap out another number and speak to someone in rapid Greek.

This was it. *The end.* Zac must hate her.

"I'm so sorry." There was a deep, hoarse note in his voice that made her heart twist. "The tabloids are going to crucify you. It's going to be hell on earth for you."

She blinked, struggling to comprehend what he was saying. His shoes came into her line of vision and her head jerked up. "*For me?* What about you?"

He shrugged. "I will survive."

He would, too. Zac had that strong inner sense of self—it was what set him apart, what made him clearly a man among men. Here stood a man who all his life had been groomed for a position of power and followed the path that had been ordained for him from the minute he had been born. A man who had never set a foot wrong…until *she* had wrecked it all for him. Why should he pay the price for her mistakes?

She stared at his shoes, wishing a hole would open up in the carpet below through which she could sink. There was no doubt in her mind that Zac was going to pay the price, going to be humiliated in front of his peers, his business connections. The Kyriakos name was about to be dragged through the press.

It was all her fault.

At last she lifted her head and scanned his beloved features, taking in the harsh lines of strain around his mouth. The dark rings under his eyes only added to his appeal, giving him a dangerous glamour. "You must wish that you'd never set eyes on me."

Zac gave her a long, unfathomable look. "It is done."

He hadn't denied it. There was no doubt in her mind that he wished he'd never met her. Not that she could blame him. She'd brought him nothing but trouble. The thought hurt desperately.

Finally she asked, "Who leaked the story?"

Zac shook his head, and his eyes turned a dark, stormy green. "I don't know. I've already advised my security team of the breach. Believe me, I'll have the answer to your question very shortly. And when I get my hands on the bastard's wretched neck, his life will not be worth living."

The set of his mouth was grim.

A brief instant of pity for the culprit swept Pandora. It had to be an insider. Briefly she considered Stavros. She glanced at Zac, took in his fierce expression and decided against raising Stavros's name. Surely Stavros wouldn't be so stupid? He wouldn't risk his easy life married to Katy. She thought of the others she's come to know. Aki, Maria and Georgios and the rest of Zac's trusted staff and hoped none of them had betrayed him. Zac would be merciless in retribution.

The following morning Pandora wakened in the guest bedroom she'd chosen to sleep in to the sound of a commotion outside. Hurriedly, she slipped out of bed, pulled on a terry robe and crossed to the window.

Peering around the corner of the drawn drapes, she took in the photographers crowding the sidewalk and a security guard hanging out of a car, calling for the mass to disband through a loudspeaker.

Her heart sank and she ducked out of sight. So much for Zac's "No comment" yesterday.

They must be headline news this morning. Zac would be cursing her as he tried to control the notoriety the publicity must be causing him, his family and Kyriakos Shipping.

She showered and dressed hastily. The mirror revealed that she looked smart and composed in a pair of oyster trousers with a silver-blue silk blouse. By the time she'd slipped on a string of pearls, a pair of high heels and make-up, no one would detect the shame and misery beneath the mask.

Now she simply had to free Zac from the trouble she'd caused him.

Unzipping her purse, she pulled out her cell phone and perched herself on the corner of the bed.

"Daddy? Are you there?" Pandora asked as the line crackled.

There was brief silence, then her father's sigh came heavily over the line. "I've heard, Pandora. The story has already been picked up by the evening news down here. Is it true? Did you lose your virginity to Zac's brother-in-law?"

"Dad, I need to get out of Zac's life. I need to come home." Maybe if she hid at the end of the world and didn't have to meet Zac's angry gaze, she'd find the strength to cope with the horror of having her face infamously plastered over the world's newspapers. Of coming to terms with the fact that she was not the bride Zac Kyriakos needed—or loved.

"Is it true?"

What was the point in obfuscating? It had all happened so long ago. "Yes."

Even across the line she could hear her father release his breath. "You lost your virginity at seventeen to the man who is now your brother-in-law?"

It sounded so sordid. Pandora bit back a sob. "Yes."

"Poor Zac!"

Her father's exclamation cut her to the quick. She'd been worried about what it was all doing to Zac. Perhaps selfishly, she'd expected a little sympathy from her father.

"What about *me?* You and Zac cooked this marriage up between you. I didn't know I was supposed to be a virgin— not that the loss of my virginity was the kind of thing I would tell you about. *I fell in love with Zac.* Only to find out that he married me for my nonexistent virginity, that he didn't love me at all! I've been a silly little goose—twice over." All the disappointment of the past weeks spilled from her.

Silence met her outburst. Pandora could picture her father standing beside his leather-top desk at High Ridge, his face stern. A wave of longing swept her. "Daddy—"

"Pandora, I introduced Zac to you for the best reasons in the world. Zac needed a wife—he's a man I respect and admire. I leaped at the chance that you two might suit. You're my only child. I've always worried about you. About the unscrupulous men who might target you for your fortune. Your home is with Zac."

"How can Zac want me anymore? I've been nothing but trouble to him." A sob escaped her throat. "But you're right. I can't leave him to weather this crisis alone. Thank you, Daddy." Pandora said a subdued goodbye and made her way downstairs. From the windows beside the staircase it was clear that the town house was under siege, reporters thronging against the gate.

She shuddered in horror. They were after photos of the scandalous Kyriakos virgin bride. *Soiled goods.* Stavros's words taunted her. It was what the tabloids would be screaming, too.

Pausing in the archway to the sitting room, her heart missed a beat as she took in Zac's tall, lean frame. With a sense of inevitability, she saw the paper in his hands.

"Let me see that."

Poker-faced, he tried to hide it behind his back, but Pandora would have none of it. "I want to read what they say about me."

He handed it to her with a sigh. "Don't let it get to you. So much is lies."

The headlines were a thousand times worse than she'd anticipated, and for a moment Pandora wished she had fled back to her father, to the sanctuary of High Ridge.

"Zac duped by fake virgin," proclaimed one. And "Marriage turns tycoon into fool," screamed another.

"What impact is all this going to have on the company?" she asked, her hand over her mouth.

"The share price has already hiccupped." He must have read something of the devastation that ripped at her insides, because he said dismissively, "It will be a temporary thing. It will stabilise. We'll see what happens by the close of day on Wall Street."

"I'm so sorry," she said in a small voice.

"Try not to think about it," Zac advised. "We will get through this."

"I wish there was something I could do," she said.

But Zac had already picked up the remote and started flicking through the news channels, a frown on his face, and he didn't answer.

By the end of the day she was a wreck. She crawled into her bed—alone—unable to face Zac after the ignominy of the day's headlines.

She half hoped that Zac might come find her, make love to her, help her forget what was happening.

As she waited, tense and distressed, thoughts spun wildly inside her head. Finally, a long time later, she started to think clearly.

Zac would not come to her tonight. Zac could not stay married to her after this. He would have to divorce her. He had no choice.

And as she faced that truth, loss ripped through her. Despite the heat, she shivered against the cool sheets. The future that lay ahead would be bleak and a little scary without Zac.

But she still had tonight. And tomorrow night. And all the other nights until Zac asked her to release him from their vows. Those nights ahead offered a respite from the emptiness that she knew would dog her in the months to come. Could she do it? Could she climb into Zac's bed?

Was that something she could do for Zac—give him a few nights of mind-blowing pleasure? Would that go part of the way to easing the chaos she'd caused in his life?

Quaking a little with apprehension, she crawled out of bed and made her way to the cupboard into which a maid had unpacked her clothes. With trembling hands Pandora lifted out a wisp of pale silver silk that she'd bought for her honeymoon but never worn. It took less than a minute to shuck off her comfortable cotton nightie, brush her hair, spray on a little scent and don the silky garment that had been made for seduction. Her heart thudding against her ribs, she clicked off the bedroom light and stepped out into the moonlit corridor, her bare feet soundless against the thickly carpeted floor.

On reaching Zac's bedroom door she halted, her heart pounding. Could she do this? She turned the door handle and stepped into the room.

Zac was propped up against plump pillows. He glanced up, then froze. A lightning-swift look revealed his sleek, bare chest covered from the waist down by a white sheet.

"I came to say sorry." The expression on his face made Pandora conscious of exactly how little she wore, how skimpy the sexy little nightgown was and how provocative she must appear. She swallowed nervously. "Maybe this isn't such a good idea."

Zac's eyes flared, turning his face starkly male. "Come here."

Nine

For a moment Pandora looked as if she were about to flee, and Zac discovered that he was not going to let that happen.

Suddenly he didn't give a damn why she was here, that this might be about guilt for lying to him or penance for the headlines. It didn't matter. All he cared about was that she was here. That he would be able to kiss her, feel the touch of her skin against his, feel her silken walls closing against his hardening erection.

He lifted the covers. "Come," he said hoarsely.

She was across the room in a second and slid under the sheet, taking care not to touch him.

Rolling onto his side and raising himself onto an elbow, Zac faced his wife. She lay on her back, stiff and silent, staring at the ceiling. Her skin was luminous, her profile delicate and her pale hair gleamed against the snowy sheets. "You are the most beautiful woman in the whole world." Reaching out his hand, he stroked her shoulder. The shoelace tie of her nightgown fell away and she turned her head. Her eyes were wide and something sparked inside the silver depths as their gazes connected.

The heat started deep in Zac's stomach, spreading outward, pushing through his bloodstream…into his head. Never had he wanted a woman this much. Never had he felt the tenderness…the pain…that this woman roused in him.

Her lips parted. He dipped his head. Her mouth was warm and moist and so, so soft. His tongue touched hers, smooth and intoxicating, while his hand pushed the bit of silver silk down the length of her body, his fingers lingering against her skin. With a groan, Zac shifted closer, until his torso brushed her breasts.

Zac brought his hands up, spanned her rib cage, and his blunt fingertips sank into soft flesh. She moaned, stretched, and her breasts rose into proud, taut mounds, enticing him.

"You're beautiful." He reached out to touch. The peaks hardened, nudging his fingers, and he bent his head to take a pale pink tip into his mouth. Pandora gasped out loud and arched under him. His tongue flicked across the tight tip. She shuddered and moved restlessly against him.

His body responded, blood pumping through his veins in a hot rush. He could feel his erection pulsing, ready for her. Then her hand slipped between them, closed around him, holding him.

Zac raised his head. "Are you sure?" he gritted out.

"Oh, yes."

Her fingers started to caress him, sliding along his length, driving him wild.

His breath caught. "*Don't.* I can't hold back."

But she ignored him. Her hand moved. Zac didn't know whether to curse or kiss her.

She moved beneath him, positioning him so that he could feel the hot heat of her against him. He moaned, surged forward. And then he was inside her. Home, where he belonged. Clenching his teeth, forcing himself to slow down, Zac drew away and sank slowly back into her. Her body was tight and hot and utterly irresistible.

"Zeus, this is good."

He moved again.

And again.

She murmured something and wiggled her hips against him. He felt her tongue slick and smooth against his neck. The little licks sent shivers exploding through him. He drove his hips forward. Pandora responded instantly, her body arched against his, her breath ragged against his neck.

To slow the tightening tension, he slid out, waited a heartbeat and thrust back into her. She gave a little hoarse cry. Then her tongue was back, touching him, tantalising him, circling his earlobe, her hot breath sending adrenaline rocketing through him.

She whispered, "I'm almost there."

"Pandora!" The pressure spiralled up, pleasure and still more pressure until he could hold no longer, until it spun away. He let it all go and heard her gasp as he sank into her again and again, faster and faster until it all tore free.

"Now." His voice was hoarse. The spasms engulfed them, and he shuddered at the sensation.

Afterward, raising himself onto his elbows, he fought for breath. "Wow."

"Is that all you can say?" Her face glowed with desire and a hint of an emotion he'd never seen before.

He gave a broken, shaky laugh and smoothed a lock of her hair off her forehead.

"It's not over yet," she said.

But something in her tone caught his attention. Zac lifted his head. There was resignation in her eyes…and a hint of—what?—desperation? Zac's heart tightened into a band of pain inside his chest. He swallowed and stared down into her eyes, darkened to a cloudy grey and saddened by an emotion that looked suspiciously like regret.

No. She couldn't mean this to be goodbye.

"What do you mean it's not over yet?" He tried to hide his own desperation.

Her lips curved into a smile, but her eyes remained grave. "Tonight, we have tonight. And tomorrow night. And some nights beyond that. But sometime soon you're going to have to make that decision, Zac. About us. About our marriage. And I already know what it will be. Divorce. It can't be any other way."

Divorce.

The end of this magic sweetness between them. It was the last thing he wanted. He'd been raised to believe that a Kyriakos never divorced. The band inside him tightened. *It can't be any other way.* Anguish followed in the wake of her words.

Or could it? Deep inside the heart of him, something gave. For the first time in his life he didn't care about the future. About what people thought. Her past didn't matter any longer. More than anything in the world he wanted to banish the shadows from her eyes, to see her happy again.

What mattered most was that she was his. He no longer cared what people thought of the Kyriakos heir. He no longer cared about his dead grandfather's expectations—or that he might be considered a failure to the family name. He was not like his father. He would never fail his wife.

Because he had no intention of letting his bride go.

Ever.

Before he had time to ponder on the blindsiding discovery, Pandora touched him again.

"Are you ready? Or do you want to wait a while? We have all night."

Amazingly he found he was already hard again. Need surged through him and he pulled her toward him. "All night? Then let's not waste one minute." And he moved her warm, naked body over his.

When she awoke, it was morning. Zac stood beside the window, dressed in a suit, his back to her, his hands on his lean hips.

He must have heard her stir, because he turned.

"Pandora—" He started to say something, broke off. There was a sudden sense of awkwardness. "Did you have enough sleep?" he said at last. "You must be tired. It's Friday—take your time, relax, don't hurry to get up."

The memory of the night came to her. The things they'd done, the magic of their togetherness…the terrible sense of time running out. She searched his eyes, seeking answers to the questions she was too scared to ask. Is this the end? How many nights more? When do I go? Why did you have to be the man you are…and why could I not be the woman you needed?

Finally she said only, "I'm a little tired." Oh, dear God, why were they spouting banalities when she needed—

Zac's cell phone trilled.

He reached for it, glanced at the number and answered, keeping his responses short.

Pandora bit her lip. What had the press printed now?

Zac killed the line. "Katy is on her way over. She says she needs to see us. She sounded in a bad way." His gaze softened. "I'm sorry, Pandora, no chance for a lie in today. You'll need to get up and dressed."

Once downstairs, the tension in the sitting room was thick and palpable between them, the awkwardness of earlier undiminished. At last the sound of heels clicking on the marble entrance hall made Pandora look up from the book she'd been pretending to read.

Katy stood in the doorway, her face red and blotchy from crying, her heart-shaped face wearing a hurt, vulnerable expression.

Pandora shut her eyes. Katy had obviously been reading the papers. Pandora hadn't seen or spoken to Zac's sister since that awful moment on Kiranos. The last thing she needed was Katy's condemnation. Beside her she heard Zac rise to his feet. She opened her eyes to see him making his way across the room, intent on cutting Katy off.

Katy flung herself into her brother's arms. "It's terrible."

"I know." Over Katy's head Pandora read the pain in Zac's eyes. "But it will pass."

Poor Katy, having to read about her husband's lover along with everyone else. God, how many more people was that reckless one-night stand going to affect? If she could only have the time over, she'd never have done it. But she'd been seventeen, in love—or so she'd thought. Hardly surprising she'd had so little sense.

Zac had produced a hanky and was mopping up Katy's tears. But that only made Katy cry harder. "You're going to hate Stavros even more. But I *have* to tell you."

Zac froze. "What has that stupid bastard done now?"

"Zac!" Stepping back, Katy said, "Don't swear."

"Sorry, but he is a thorn in my side."

"I know," Katy wailed. "And now it will be even worse. I just found out today—a journalist called looking for him. Stavros contacted the papers, sold the story about him and Pandora."

"He did *what?*"

The fury in Zac's voice made Pandora cringe. At the expression on Katy's face, she leaped to her feet and rushed across the room. "Don't be mad at Katy. It's not her fault."

Katy fell into Pandora's arms. "I thought you'd never speak to me again. Stavros has done you such harm."

"But *you* haven't," Pandora pointed out gently. Over Katy's shoulder she caught a glimpse of Zac's stunned expression.

"I'm leaving him," Katy declared. "I never want to see him again. This time he's gone too far."

Zac closed his eyes. "I never thought you'd see sense."

"I can't believe he did this." Katy's eyes were full of bewilderment. "I knew he wasn't strong or invulnerable like you, but he's funny and he always makes me feel so… special."

"He's a lightweight, a fortune—"

Pandora shot Zac a warning look. For once he heeded it and broke off.

"I know what you think of him." Katy looked gutted. "But I thought you were wrong. I honestly, truly believed he loved me. That's why I never listened to you. And there's never been anyone else. If he'd been what you said, I thought he'd give himself away long ago."

"A bird in the hand is worth—"

"Zac," Pandora said quellingly. "Shut up."

To her amazement, he did.

Katy started to laugh—a touch hysterically. "Oh, Pandora, I love you. I don't think I've ever heard anyone tell Zac to shut up and live to tell the tale. Please never leave my brother. You're the only one who can keep him in line."

For a moment Zac looked as if he wanted to object, then he closed his mouth and shook his head. "Women," he muttered.

Pandora assessed Katy critically. It was obvious that Zac's sister had been through hell, but despite her tear-blotched face she looked composed. "Will you be okay staying alone, without Stavros? Or have you got a friend that can stay over for a few nights and keep you company? Do you want to stay here?"

"I'm staying with Stacy. She will handle my divorce. Stavros keeps calling me at home and I don't want to talk to him. Stacy's arranged for the number to be changed. But for the meantime the calls are being forwarded to her service. I've got a new cell-phone number, too. Stacy's taken my old cell phone and she's fielding the incoming calls."

"You're serious about this, aren't you?" Zac was looking at his sister as if he'd never seen her before.

"I have to be. It's going to be even harder when the baby comes."

"Baby?" Zac and Pandora spoke together.

"What baby?" Zac asked.

Katy's hand went to her mouth. "I haven't told anyone. I only found out today. We've been trying ever since that first miscarriage. I was so excited. But then I found out about Stavros selling that disgusting story—" she blinked as Pandora blanched "—sorry, Pandora. So I called Stavros and told him he shouldn't bother coming home. Not ever again."

"Did you tell Stavros about the baby?"

Katy glared at Zac. "Stavros doesn't need to know about the baby. I'm perfectly capable of raising her alone."

The eyes so like her brother's were flashing. Despite her own misery, Pandora suppressed the urge to cheer.

"You already know it's a girl?" Zac cast his sister a sharp look.

"I hope it is. I want a girl. I'm so sick of men."

Zac raised his eyebrows.

"Not you, of course—you're my brother. And I suppose once Stavros and I are divorced, the dislike of the species will fade."

Pandora suppressed the urge to laugh. It was not the right time. But Katy was on fire.

Katy sniffed and blew her nose. "I can't believe you're both being so nice to me. Stavros sold that exposé to cover gambling debts. I keep thinking I could've stopped it. He begged me to pay them. I refused. Last year, when you helped me get rid of those money lenders, Zac, I told him that it was the last time, that he needed help. I never thought my husband would stoop to this."

When Zac walked back into the sitting room after seeing Katy to the door, he found Pandora hunched over the tabloids, looking utterly wretched.

A twinge of pity, underscored by fury at his brother-in-law, shot through him. "Remember when you first came to Athens I said don't read the papers—they'll only upset you."

"You extracted that promise because you didn't want me reading about the speculation that you'd found a virgin bride in the remoteness of the New Zealand wilderness."

"Partly," he admitted. "But I also didn't want you reading the hurtful lies the scandal sheets print."

"Except this time it's true."

Zac blew out. "Thanks to my traitorous dog of a brother-in-law."

"And my lack of judgment three years ago. What did I ever see in Stavros?"

Zac's mouth kinked. "The impulsivity of youth." But his heart lightened. The fear that Pandora still fancied Stavros started to fade, leaving him surprisingly carefree.

"Oh, jeez!" She dropped the paper she'd been scanning. "That's disgusting."

"Don't read it." But the horror in her eyes had him reaching for the paper she'd dropped.

"They're saying that it's keeping love in the family, I'm the family whore. I feel like crawling into a hole and never coming out again. They've quoted Stavros—but it's all wrong. They're saying I met him in a scuzzy nightclub. They've even got a photo of it—it's called Wild Thing and it's famous for the wild swingers who hang out there, according to this article. But, I swear, I've never been there in my life."

Fury rose. "I'll sue. Put that rag out of business." He reached for the phone. After a short conversation with Dimitri, he dropped down on the couch beside her and gave her shoulder an awkward pat. "You're doing fine."

She buried her head in her hands. "I've besmirched your name. The sooner you get divorce proceedings under way, the better."

"I never said I wanted a divorce."

"You were thinking about it."

"I wanted time to work out what to do, how to cope with my feelings, the fact that you lied to me about your relationship with Stavros. With the story out, the damage is done. There will be no divorce."

Pandora grew still.

"It is Stavros who turned what was a private affair into a public scandal. Not you. My family has humiliated you. Believe me, I will not desert you."

Pandora peered at Zac through her laced fingers. He looked fierce and uncompromising.

"It is my responsibility to protect you." Zac sat straight and proud. If she hadn't loved him already, she would've fallen for him right that moment. This must be how his forefather's had looked when they'd ridden out and put the fear of death into the enemy while protecting those closest to them.

It shouldn't make her feel better that he was so protective of her. She was a modern woman. Feeling this way was positively archaic.

"After all that has happened, why do you feel the need to protect me?"

He looked trapped. "Because you are my wife."

"But why risk what it will do to you, to your profile?"

"I will survive." He smiled, then his eyes grew serious. "It will be better if we stay together. For appearances. My PR department will sell it to the media that we love each other, that our love is pure and that we respect the sanctity of our marriage. They will be convincing that your virginity is not an issue, the Kyriakos heir has found true love and will be married forever."

"But that's a lie. You don't love me," she objected, incredibly tempted to give in to the spin he was creating.

Zac shrugged. "My PR department will create the illusion of love."

His words brought her back to reality. Of course this wasn't about them, about true love. Last night's lovemaking would've made no difference to Zac. He was too in control for emotion to rule him. Her shoulders sagged, and instantly she forced herself to straighten her spine. Zac had analysed the situation and come up with a solution.

As little as she wanted such a marriage, how could she refuse? She owed Zac her support. Her place was by his side. After all, he was stuck in this quandary because of her.

"It sounds like it could work. Although it would've been easier if we'd really loved each other," she said a touch wistfully.

"Many marriages survive without love." Zac's expression revealed no emotion. "You've told me often enough you hate me. Love or hate, I married you—you are my responsibility. Especially now that my brother-in-law has defiled you in public."

Three things struck Pandora. First, Stavros had ensured that Zac would sacrifice himself, his name, because of his misguided all-important sense of honour. Secondly, Zac had already decided a marriage for the sake of appearances would take care of everything. And thirdly, Zac believed—wrongly—that she hated him.

Suddenly it was very important to rectify that misunderstanding. The trick was to do so without revealing what he meant to her. "I don't hate you," she said softly.

But Zac was already talking. "There are other things that are important—children, business, having someone to confide in."

"Children?" Pandora's heart started to ache. *Zac's children.* He would love his children, but not their mother. "So you intend us to have—" she swallowed "—children?"

"Of course." The searing look he gave her made her toes curl.

"Even though your nose will forever be rubbed in the fact that Stavros had me first?"

His jaw grew rock-hard. "We will not talk about that."

"But, Zac, the media will never let us forget it."

"I will take care of the media. We will fight fire with fire," he replied. "They are going to devour our story of true love."

Ten

The weekend passed in a haze of English drizzle, but even that did not deter the media siege outside the town house. Zac's security firm had brought in extra guards with fierce Dobermans on short leashes to patrol the fence perimeter, lest any story-driven newsperson venture onto the grounds.

A dinner out on Saturday night in a wildly popular restaurant where Pandora and Zac were snapped staring into each other's eyes and a supposedly spontaneous scoop while she and Zac strolled through Hyde Park tucked under one umbrella, their hands linked, were part of the PR plan to sow the seeds that this was a love match.

By Monday morning the tenor of the stories had started to change. Pandora no longer read them and tried to get on with her own life, but even she could not help being aware of the difference as the Kyriakos publicity machine started to take effect. She couldn't help thinking that Zac must be ecstatic that the blip in the Kyriakos share price had passed.

By the time Zac disappeared to the London office of Kyriakos Shipping, Pandora felt nothing but relief.

Determined to shake off the blues and make the best of her marriage, she arranged to meet Katy for lunch. Zac's chauffeur employed a range of offensive driving tactics to shake off the more persistent reporters and finally delivered Pandora to an exclusive department store where she was to join up with Katy. Hidden behind a disguise of overlarge sunglasses, with her giveaway pale hair firmly secured under a head scarf, Pandora helped Katy shop for some maternity blouses and dresses even though it was still too early in Katy's pregnancy for her to need them.

As they looked at baby clothes, Pandora couldn't help thinking about her discussion with Zac about children being a natural consequence of marriage. An unexpected pang of emotion floored her as she held up a tiny boys' T-shirt.

Her and Zac's baby.

Would her love be enough to hold them together? She didn't know. And he didn't even know she loved him. Should she tell him? One thing that had kept them apart had been her lie about Stavros. And deceiving Zac about the way she felt about him didn't seem like the right thing to do any longer. Not since she'd discovered he thought she hated him.

Biting her lip, she folded the little T-shirt up and put it back on the shelf and went in search of Katy.

By the time she arrived home she'd decided that it was vital for her to tell Zac the truth about how she felt about him. Even though he would never love her back, he deserved the truth.

But that evening Zac worked so late that Pandora was asleep by the time he came home. Tuesday came and her nerve gave out. She was dreading telling him how she felt about him, certain that it was going to be an exercise in humiliation. Not that Zac would intend it to be so, but how could he ever love her back?

On Wednesday morning, Pandora vowed she would tell Zac this evening. But when he called in the late afternoon to let her know that his meeting was running later than expected, the coward in her was relieved.

She was watching a video when the doorbell rang late that night.

The sound of male voices in the entrance hall drew her out of the sitting room, and she paused abruptly at the sight of Stavros arguing with Aki in the doorway, hands flying everywhere.

"Pandora." Stavros caught sight of her and shouldered Aki aside.

"Zac isn't here."

"Then I need to talk to you. Tell your guard dog it's okay."

Aki wore a disapproving expression. "*Kyria,* he should not be here. He's been drinking."

Raising a hand to silence Aki and frowning slightly, Pandora said, "Why don't you ring Zac in the morning? Set up a time to see him then?"

"It's about Katy."

The baby. Concern shot through Pandora. But Katey should be with Stacy. "Is Katy all right?"

"Can I at least come in?"

Ignoring Aki's disapproval, she nodded and motioned him through to the sitting room. Picking up the remote, she flicked off the television and positioned herself on the footrest in front of it.

Stavros collapsed onto one of the plump brown chesterfield sofas.

"What's the matter with Katy?" Pandora asked.

"She's booted me out. She wants a divorce."

Pandora gaped at him. "That's why you turn up here—" she glanced at her watch "—at ten o'clock on a Wednesday night? To tell me your wife's left you? It's hardly news that comes as any surprise."

"I can't reach my wife." He lurched to his feet. "Zac won't take my calls at his office. I want you to help me get Katy back."

"If Katy's left you, that's her decision. Nothing I can say will change it."

"Talk to your husband. He can influence Katy."

"Oh, no. I'm not getting in the middle of a marital quarrel. You got yourself into this by selling that damn story, you get yourself out." All her anger poured out in a torrent.

"You self-righteous little bitch. If you don't help me, I'm going to call up my reporter friend, tell him I've got another story for him."

"You wouldn't!" But fear burst inside her. She was never going to be free of Stavros's tentacles. He had a hold over her and he was never going to let go. Zac would be humiliated all over again. Would it never end?

Stavros came closer, triumph contorting his features. "He's eager for details. I'll tell him what you're wearing, how you lay down for me on—" he glanced around "—Zac's fancy rug beneath that painting he likes so much."

"I'm not listening to this." She jumped up. Aki was right—Stavros had been drinking. A lot. She could smell the alcohol fumes.

But before she got past, Stavros grabbed her. "I'll tell him how you squealed with passion as I—"

"Get away from me!"

"Didn't I warn you not to come near my wife?" The soft, dangerous lash of Zac's voice made Pandora jump. He stood on the threshold clad in a dark suit, holding a black briefcase, and his stillness was oddly threatening.

Instantly Stavros let her go and started backing away. "She asked me to touch her. She's hot for me."

Damn Stavros. Pandora knew she must look dishevelled. She pushed her fringe out of her eyes with shaking hands. "Zac—"

Zac's eyes had turned a flat, unforgiving green drained of all emotion. Ice. Cold and hard and freezingly remote. "You are no longer welcome in my home, Politsis. Get out. You'll find a cab waiting at the door. Be thankful that you are my sister's husband or I would call the police and lay charges of assault."

"I never touched you," Stavros spat out.

"But you touched my wife. And that is something I cannot forgive."

A flash of naked terror contorted Stavros's face. "I'm going." But as he reached the door, he turned. "But you're going to regret this."

Zac laughed, a chilling sound without amusement. "Do your worst, Politsis. You'll regret anything you do to harm any Kyriakos—and that includes my sister. Stay away from us. Get your own life. Or be ready to face the consequences."

* * *

Stavros departed in a screech of tires, ignoring the cab parked at the front door.

"I was so scared." Pandora decided to go for broke.

Zac came toward her, his arms outstretched. "I should have turned him to pulp for frightening you."

"I wasn't afraid of Stavros. Or, rather, I was terrified of what Stavros was threatening because I thought it meant the end of everything between us. But I was more afraid that you might believe Stavros when he said—" She broke off.

"When he said that you were hot for him?"

She nodded despairingly. "I was afraid you might think I'd betrayed you and considered sleeping with him."

Colour rushed into Zac's face. "Never. You're my wife."

Relief made Pandora go limp. "He came looking for you—apparently you wouldn't take his calls. He tried to force me to help him get Katy back. I'm worried for her."

Zac made for the phone, and Pandora heard him giving someone the address where Katy was staying, telling them to keep a look out for Stavros.

"So that's how you knew he was here. The security company called."

"Yes. They've been keeping close surveillance. But not because I didn't trust you with Stavros," he added hastily when he realised how she might construe his words. "I was worried some overzealous reporter might try get into the house."

Pandora knew that she and Zac needed to talk. Butterflies fluttered in her stomach. Finally she plucked up the courage to say, "Zac, there's something I need to tell you."

He turned to look at her. "What?"

"I've been thinking about why I married you." He looked startled and about to speak, but she held up a hand. "Wait, hear me out. A gorgeous, incredibly handsome guy who could have any woman in the world, and I was so dumb I never asked why you'd chosen *me*."

Zac opened his mouth.

"I'm not finished. I stayed married even when I discovered I wasn't the bride you needed because—" she hesitated "—because the biggest mistake I made was falling in love with you."

"You love me?"

"Of course I love you, Zac. And that's part of the problem. Because you're Zac Kyriakos. Too perfect to be true." More quietly she added, "The only mistake you've ever made in your perfect life was to marry me."

"I thought you hated me." He looked dazed.

"Zac? Are you listening?"

He simply stared at her, looking poleaxed. Pandora suppressed the urge to laugh at the ridiculous notion that any woman would hate him.

The phone shrilled into the charged silence. Zac didn't move. So Pandora started to rise to get it.

"It's almost midnight. Ignore it," Zac said urgently. "We need to finish this."

The ringing stopped. An awkward pause stretched between them. Before they could resume the conversation, a knock sounded on the door.

"Yes?" Zac demanded impatiently as Aki entered the room. "What is it?"

"It's your sister."

"Tell her I'm busy," Zac bit out. Then, softening his tone, he added, "I'll call her back. Later—much later."

Aki looked worried. "She says it's an emergency. Mr. Politsis has had an accident. He's in hospital, in a critical condition."

By the time Zac and Pandora arrived at the hospital, the news hounds, scenting a story, were already clustered outside the main entrance. His arm around her shoulder, Zac shouldered his way through the small crowd, while hospital security and Zac's bodyguards pushed the more aggressive reporters back.

Upstairs, Katy was pacing the plush carpet of the private waiting room, holding her stomach. Stavros was still in surgery, she told them in a thin voice.

"He arrived and started banging on Stacy's front door, yelling threats. We wouldn't let him in. Then two of your security guys arrived, told him to calm down. He stormed off." Katy swallowed visibly. "Next thing, the police called. Stavros had been speeding, driving recklessly. They gave chase. He ploughed his car into a wall. They said he was in hospital, that it was critical." Katy started to cry. "And now the doctors aren't telling me anything."

"I'll get some details." Zac patted her shoulder and disappeared out the door like a man on a mission.

"It's the waiting, it's killing me—" Katy stopped and looked horrified. "Oh, God, I don't mean that."

Pandora hastened to her side. Katy flung her arms around Pandora. "What's going to happen?"

"Hush." Pandora hugged Katy. "We'll stay with you for as long as you need us."

"I was so pleased about the baby. I wanted a baby so badly. I thought it would make everything right, force

Stavros to settle down even though he was never that keen on having kids. But then Stavros did that awful thing…" Katy covered her face with her hands and her shoulders started to shake. "I'm going to find a restroom. I need to wash my face."

Zac returned just after Katy had left, his face somber. "Where's Katy?"

"She's gone to freshen up." Pandora examined his face. "Is the news bad?"

He sank down on the chair beside her and took her hands. "Stavros has lost a lot of blood and the doctors are worried about the head injuries he sustained."

"Does that mean he's suffered brain damage?"

"They're not saying too much yet. Someone will be along as soon as they get out of surgery with an update." Zac sighed heavily. "All day I have wanted to be alone with you, and now that I am, I can only think that a couple of hours ago I wished that Stavros would disappear out of our lives. I didn't want to think about him…with you. Now he may die." His grip tightened on her hands. "And I can't stop thinking that I wished it on him."

"It's not your fault. You didn't cause his accident." Pandora slid her hands out of his hold and placed them around his shoulders, comforting him. "You didn't get him drunk or force him to drive like a delinquent. Jeez, you even ordered him a cab."

He turned into her arms and rested his head against her hair. "Thank you."

"You're too hard on yourself."

He took a deep breath. "I wanted you to be mine. Only mine."

"Zac—"

"I *am* a barbarian, you see. I'm not the perfect man you think I am—that I've always striven to be." His voice was full of torment.

"Zac, listen to me. I am yours. Only yours. And you're utterly perfect for me." Her arms crept around his neck and she held him tight. "You're not alone, you know."

"What do you mean?" Zac raised his head and stared at her.

"You weren't the only one who wished Stavros away— I told you he was dead. I think I hoped he was. It was far easier that way." Pandora gave him a shaky ghost of a smile.

Guilt. She felt guilty about sleeping with Stavros years ago. Zac looked at her carefully, saw the wariness in her eyes, the fine lines of strain around her mouth. No, he didn't want her experiencing guilt. Hell, she hadn't known him back then—hadn't known he even existed.

"I owe you an apology." He lifted his hand to cup her cheek. "I've never considered myself a possessive man, yet where you are concerned I find I am. I disliked the idea of you sleeping with Stavros—" he paused, searching for words, couldn't find any way to say it except for the truth "—because I was jealous."

"Jealous?" She stared at him. "But, for heaven's sake, Zac, why would you be jealous of Stavros? He isn't a patch of the man you are. You are so much more than Stavros could ever be."

So much more than Stavros could ever be. And just like that, the corrosive bitterness inside him evaporated.

He gave her cheek a last stroke and couldn't help marvelling at how fortunate he was to have Pandora. A few minutes later, when Katy came back looking a little more composed, he was doubly relieved to have Pandora at his side while he broke the news about Stavros to his sister.

Zac drew her into the circle. "You know, whatever happens, we'll be there for you and the baby."

Katy nodded. "That's what's keeping me strong."

It was six hours later before they heard that Stavros had survived the surgery and the internal bleeding had been stanched. He'd been moved to intensive care and would be monitored through the night. But the chances of permanent brain damage were looking increasingly likely.

Katy cried a little more, and Pandora and Zac did their best to support her as she started to come to terms with the shock.

"We're here for you," Zac said. "Whatever you want to do, we will support you."

Katy flung her arms around him. "You're the best brother in the world. What would I ever do without you?" She wanted to call Dimitri and Stacy with an update. Zac called his cousins, Tariq and Angelo, and informed them of the situation. Both insisted on speaking to Katy. Both men wanted to fly out immediately. Zac dissuaded them.

Stacy arrived and insisted on taking Katy back to her apartment. There was nothing left but for Zac and Pandora to go home.

Forty minutes later, Zac followed Pandora into the town house and bolted the front door.

Pandora yawned. "I'm tired. I'm going to bed."

"Oh, no, you're not. We have a discussion to finish." Zac caught her arm. She stiffened in his grasp, but he took heart from the fact that she didn't pull away.

"It's been a hell of a day." Then, after a beat, he added very quietly, "I need you."

"Why?"

He closed his eyes. He was going to have to lay himself bare.

"I love you." He made the mistake of opening his eyes. Pandora was shaking her head from side to side.

Zeus, had he made a huge, irrevocable mistake? Had she been joking earlier? Trying to teach him a lesson by pretending to love him? No. He dismissed his wild panic. Pandora would not do that. Not even to him.

"You love me?" she said slowly, disbelievingly, and came closer until she was standing in front of him, looking up at him.

"Yes." He waited, frozen, for her next move.

"*Yes*. That's all you can say?" Her voice rose and she jabbed him in the chest with her finger.

A huge wave of relief washed through him. She cared. "I thought *yes* was the most valued word in this kind of exchange."

Her silver eyes flashed. "Since when did you decide you loved me?"

"Pandora…" he said gently, putting his arms around her shoulders and leading her to the sitting room. He pulled her down on the sofa beside him and turned to face her. "I'm going to be honest with you. I struggled to find a bride. There were many candidates. But none of them were right."

"Why not?"

He shrugged. "I don't know how to explain it. But I kept putting marriage off. And then suddenly one day I realized that the years were passing and it was starting to look like

I would never find a suitable wife. I grew desperate. I met your father and he told me about you. You sounded perfect. Sweet and sheltered."

She made a growling sound.

He laughed, pulled her close and kissed her on the top of her head before setting her away from him. "Then I met you. You blew all my preconceptions away. You were so young. So beautiful with your pale hair and ethereal silver eyes. You looked like everything the Kyriakos virgin should be. But it wasn't just your looks. You were smart. Funny. And I wanted you."

"That's not love. That's lust at first sight."

"Maybe." Zac looked sheepish. "But you had my full attention. I left, but I couldn't stop thinking about you. I kept sneaking back to see you. I couldn't wait to have you. But you were a virgin—or so I believed, and I had no reason to doubt it—so I had to marry you first.

"When you came to Athens…that week was the week from hell. I couldn't touch you because I was terrified once I did, I wouldn't be able to stop. Our wedding night was my every fantasy come true."

"But the next morning…"

"I was furious that you wanted to leave me. I knew I couldn't let that happen. I had to convince you to stay."

"So you kidnapped me!"

"I'm sorry." Remorse darkened his eyes. "Then everything spun out of control. When I discovered you weren't a virgin…I still couldn't let you go. I was prepared to keep that our secret, anything to keep you. But even then I didn't realize what was happening. I thought it was just—" He broke off.

"Just sex?" A small smile played around her mouth.

He nodded. "That day in the sea, when you told me that you no longer wanted to leave…and what followed…I thought I was losing my mind. It was so good. But Katy and Stavros barged in and suddenly it looked like I was going to lose you anyway. I couldn't think straight. I'd never felt such fear. I still hadn't realized I loved you. All I knew was that something had changed. My head told me that the marriage couldn't survive, but my heart knew I couldn't bear to let you go. I didn't care what it would mean. I had to keep you by my side, but I needed you to *want* to stay. I needed you to love me."

"And you thought I hated you."

He sighed. "I could live with the fact that you weren't a virgin. I realised I was a man in my own right. It didn't matter who my ancestors were. It didn't matter why my grandfather's expectations were. What I couldn't live with was the fact that you hated me. That, I considered a failure."

"I'm sorry. That was not your failure. It was my own frustration and self-preservation. I loved you. I was torn apart when I discovered you'd only married me because you thought I was a virgin. And when you took me to Kiranos, I wanted to hurt you, make you pay. I acted like a brat." She peered at him from behind her hair. "Forgive me?"

He took her into his arms. "Will you forgive me for forcing you to come with me to Kiranos, for forcing you onto the helicopter? I felt terrible when I learned about your mother."

"I forgive you." She leaned forward and pressed a quick kiss against his mouth.

"It was after the story about you and Stavros broke in the papers and I saw your anguish at what was being said that I realized I loved you." His eyes held a glow. "I wanted to protect you, keep you safe from the scandal. When you came to me that night, I knew I loved you. It was a hell of a thing for me to come to terms with."

"What a lot of time we've wasted."

Could he expect Pandora to put up with the pressures of his world, the hunger of the press? They'd caused her so much harm already, made her so unhappy. He looked into her clear, silvery eyes, at the firm chin, and he knew that he had to give her a chance. It was her choice to make…not his.

"You have to be sure you can live with me."

"I am sure."

"You've seen what my life is like. How scary my family can be—even when they mean best. You've seen how obsessive the paparazzi can be. None of that is ever going to go away. Can you live with that?"

"You know, the first thing I ever noticed about you was how sexy your mouth is." Pandora touched his mouth with her fingertip. "Made for sin, I thought."

"Be serious." But Zac felt the heat uncoiling inside him.

"I am serious. Very serious." She drew a line across his lip. "You know what? I don't care about the family or the media. Nothing matters as long as I have you." But when she glanced at him, her eyes clouded. "But what are you going to do every time the papers run a story about my relationship with Stavros? Can you survive it?"

"In future I'll follow my own advice not to read the papers—except for the business pages." He licked at her tantalising finger, tasting the perfume of her skin. "And I'll have you. That makes up for whatever the media cares to throw at me. Which reminds me…I meant to tell you, the share price is up. It looks like everyone loves the idea of the Kyriakos heir finding true love."

"That's fantastic news." Pandora looked radiant. "Enough to make me consider forgiving the media for what I went through." She paused. "You did say you were going to buy a property in New Zealand, near High Ridge Station? We can always disappear down there. And when things get really bad, there's always Kiranos. I can cope with the helicopter ride as long as you are there to hold my hand. We can hide out there. No one will find us. I mean, there's not even cell-phone contact."

Zac started to smile. "You didn't try your cell phone on Kiranos, did you?"

"No. Why?"

"Because you would've found that it worked." Zac couldn't help laughing at her expression of outrage. "My wife says I've been wasting time." Hoisting her into his arms, he rose to his feet. "So I daren't waste a single moment more."

Pandora gave an unladylike snort. "Is this about getting me into bed?"

He kissed her nose. "Yes. But it's not only about making love, it's about holding you close to my side all through the night."

"Okay."

Zac's head reared back in disbelief. "*Okay?* No arguments? You accept the fact that I'm going to carry you away to my bed just like that?"

"Our bed," she corrected. "And there are conditions…."

"What?" Zac gazed at the woman he loved with a good

dose of wariness. She was no pushover, and he suspected she knew she had the upper hand, whatever she wanted. "What do you want?"

"When we get back to Greece, I want you to take me to meet that Pano guy who runs Kyriakos Cruises—I have some great ideas for the South Pacific route. And after that, you can show me that little church next door to your house that your ancestor built, and I want to renew our vows. On my birthday in ten days' time. Just you and me. This time I want to be sure that our love for each other is out in the open. No more secrets between us."

He tightened his arms and made for the door, heading for the stairs. "Anything. Anything you want, *agapi*." And there was no hint of mockery in his voice as he added, "You are my bride, my true and only love, for all my life."

Stop Press

Kyriakos Heir Finds True Love

Zac Kyriakos announced today that both his marriage and the Kyriakos Shipping Corporation are stronger than ever. "The secret is true love," he told reporters, holding his new bride close. "I love my wife. The prophecy that the Kyriakos heir requires a virgin bride to find true love has been proved false. This marriage will last forever."

* * * * *

Look for the next book in Tessa Radley's
BILLIONAIRE HEIRS *triology,*
THE APOLLONIDES MISTRESS SCANDAL,
on sale this October from Silhouette Desire.

![Silhouette Desire logo]

There was only one man for the job—
an impossible-to-resist maverick
she knew she didn't dare fall for.

MAVERICK
(#1827)

BY *NEW YORK TIMES*
BESTSELLING AUTHOR
JOAN HOHL

"Will You Do It for One Million Dollars?"

Any other time, Tanner Wolfe would have balked at being
hired by a woman. Yet Brianna Stewart was desperate to
engage the infamous bounty hunter. The price was just
high enough to gain Tanner's interest…Brianna's beauty
definitely strong enough to keep it. But he wasn't about
to allow her to tag along on his mission. He worked
alone. Always had. Always would. However, he'd never
confronted a more determined client than Brianna. She
wasn't taking no for an answer—not about anything.

Perhaps a million-dollar bounty was not the only thing
this maverick was about to gain….

Look for MAVERICK

Available October 2007 wherever you buy books.

Ria Sterling has the gift—or is it a curse?—
of seeing a person's future in his or her
photograph. Unfortunately, when detective
Carrick Jones brings her a missing person's
case, she glimpses his partner's ID—and
sees imminent murder. And when her vision
comes true, Ria becomes the prime suspect.
Carrick isn't convinced this beautiful woman
committed the crime...but does he believe
she has the special powers to solve it?

Look for

Seeing Is Believing

by

Kate Austin

Available October
wherever you buy books.

HARLEQUIN®
NeXt™

HARLEQUIN®

Mediterranean NIGHTS™

Sail aboard the luxurious Alexandra's Dream *and* experience glamour, romance, mystery and revenge!

Coming in October 2007...

AN AFFAIR TO REMEMBER

by

Karen Kendall

When Captain Nikolas Pappas first fell in love with Helena Stamos, he was a penniless deckhand and she was the daughter of a shipping magnate. But he's never forgiven himself for the way he left her—and fifteen years later, he's determined to win her back.

Though the attraction is still there, Helena is hesitant to get involved. Nick left her once...what's to stop him from doing it again?

www.eHarlequin.com

HM38964

REQUEST YOUR FREE BOOKS!

2 FREE NOVELS PLUS 2 FREE GIFTS!

Passionate, Powerful, Provocative!

YES! Please send me 2 FREE Silhouette Desire® novels and my 2 FREE gifts. After receiving them, if I don't wish to receive any more books, I can return the shipping statement marked "cancel." If I don't cancel, I will receive 6 brand-new novels every month and be billed just $3.80 per book in the U.S., or $4.47 per book in Canada, plus 25¢ shipping and handling per book and applicable taxes, if any*. That's a savings of almost 15% off the cover price! I understand that accepting the 2 free books and gifts places me under no obligation to buy anything. I can always return a shipment and cancel at any time. Even if I never buy another book from Silhouette, the two free books and gifts are mine to keep forever.

225 SDN EEXJ   326 SDN EEXU

Name	(PLEASE PRINT)	
Address		Apt.
City	State/Prov.	Zip/Postal Code

Signature (if under 18, a parent or guardian must sign)

Mail to the **Silhouette Reader Service™:**
IN U.S.A.: P.O. Box 1867, Buffalo, NY 14240-1867
IN CANADA: P.O. Box 609, Fort Erie, Ontario L2A 5X3

Not valid to current Silhouette Desire subscribers.

Want to try two free books from another line?
Call 1-800-873-8635 or visit www.morefreebooks.com.

* Terms and prices subject to change without notice. NY residents add applicable sales tax. Canadian residents will be charged applicable provincial taxes and GST. This offer is limited to one order per household. All orders subject to approval. Credit or debit balances in a customer's account(s) may be offset by any other outstanding balance owed by or to the customer. Please allow 4 to 6 weeks for delivery.

Your Privacy: Silhouette is committed to protecting your privacy. Our Privacy Policy is available online at www.eHarlequin.com or upon request from the Reader Service. From time to time we make our lists of customers available to reputable firms who may have a product or service of interest to you. If you would prefer we not share your name and address, please check here. ☐

SDES07

HARLEQUIN®
Super Romance®

Welcome to our newest miniseries, about five
poker players and the women who love them!

Texas Hold'em
When it comes to love, the stakes are high

Beginning October 2007 with

THE BABY GAMBLE

by USA TODAY *bestselling author*

Tara Taylor Quinn
#1446

Desperate to have a baby, Annie Kincaid
turns to the only man she trusts, her ex-husband,
Blake Smith, and asks him to father her child.

Also watch for:

BETTING ON SANTA *by Debra Salonen* November 2007
GOING FOR BROKE *by Linda Style* December 2007
DEAL ME IN *by Cynthia Thomason* January 2008
TEXAS BLUFF *by Linda Warren* February 2008

Look for THE BABY GAMBLE *by* USA TODAY
bestselling author Tara Taylor Quinn.

Available October 2007 wherever you buy books.

www.eHarlequin.com

HSR71446

ATHENA FORCE

Heart-pounding romance and thrilling adventure.

A deadly masquerade

As an undercover asset for the FBI, mafia princess
Sasha Bracciali can deceive and improvise at a
moment's notice. But when she's cut off from
everything she knows, including her FBI-agent
lover, Sasha realizes her deceptions have masked
a painful truth: she doesn't know whom to trust.
If she doesn't figure it out quickly, her most
ambitious charade will also be her last.

Look for

CHARADE
by *Kate Donovan*

*Available in October
wherever you buy books.*

www.eHarlequin.com   AF38974

COMING NEXT MONTH

#1825 STRANDED WITH THE TEMPTING STRANGER—
Brenda Jackson
The Garrisons
He began his seduction with secrets and scandals in mind...but
bedding the Garrison heiress could lead to the ultimate downfall
of his hardened heart.

#1826 CAPTURED BY THE BILLIONAIRE—
Maureen Child
Reasons for Revenge
Trapped on an island resort with the man she had once jilted, she
knew her billionaire captor was about to teach her a lesson she'd
never forget.

#1827 MAVERICK—*New York Times* bestselling author
Joan Hohl
There was only one man for the job—an impossible-to-resist
maverick she didn't dare fall for.

#1828 MILLIONAIRE'S CALCULATED BABY BID—
Laura Wright
No Ring Required
She agreed to produce an heir to his financial empire...but the
secret behind this baby bargain could threaten more than their
growing attraction to one another.

#1829 THE APOLLONIDES MISTRESS SCANDAL—
Tessa Radley
Billionaire Heirs
Posing as her identical twin, she vowed revenge against her sister's
Greek lover...until she became caught in his web of seduction.

#1830 SEDUCED FOR THE INHERITANCE—
Jennifer Lewis
He would do anything to keep her from claiming his family's
inheritance...even if it meant sleeping with the one woman he
shouldn't desire....

SDCNM0907